Too nice . . .

"So," Brian said when he was done. "You want to get pizza later? Or we could rent a movie."

I stared at the bowl of pudding on his tray. "Oh, sorry, Brian. I told Lacey I'd go to the mall with her after school." I looked up at him. "You don't mind, do you?" I asked.

Brian frowned. "I thought we made plans," he said. Was I imagining things, or did he look seriously upset?

I shrugged. "We can hang out tomorrow."

"You said *today*." Brian's eyes were getting darker, I swear. "I thought we had a date," he said. "I even told the guys I couldn't practice after school today because you and I had plans."

"You did?" I asked. "Oh, Brian, you're so nice. Sometimes I wonder if I deserve you. It's like you're *too* nice."

Uh-oh. Brian's eyes were almost black now. In fact, his whole face looked like a thundercloud.

"I'm sorry, Brian," I said. "I could call Lacey and see if she can do it tomorrow."

"Don't bother," he said. He pushed back his chair and stood up. "Too nice, huh? Maybe you're right." Then he stalked over to the garbage can in the corner, dumped his tray, and stormed out of the cafeteria.

I had definitely said the wrong thing. But what's wrong with telling someone he's *nice?*

Don't miss any of the books in SWEET VALLEY JUNIOR HIGH, an exciting series from Bantam Books!

No More Mr. Nice Guy

Written by
Jamie Suzanne

Created by
FRANCINE PASCAL

BANTAM BOOKS
NEW YORK · TORONTO · LONDON · SYDNEY · AUCKLAND

RL 4, 008–012

NO MORE MR. NICE GUY
A Bantam Book / February 2001

Sweet Valley Junior High is a trademark of Francine Pascal.
Conceived by Francine Pascal.
Cover photography by Michael Segal.

Produced by 17th Street Productions,
an Alloy Online, Inc. company.
33 West 17th Street
New York, NY 10011.

ISBN: 0-553-48728-0

Visit us on the Web! www.randomhouse.com/kids

Published simultaneously in the United States and Canada

Bantam Books is an imprint of Random House Children's Books, a
division of Random House, Inc. BANTAM BOOKS and the rooster
colophon are registered trademarks of Random House, Inc. Bantam Books,
1540 Broadway, New York, New York 10036.

PRINTED IN THE UNITED STATES OF AMERICA

OPM   0 9 8 7 6 5 4 3 2 1

To Johanna McNelis

Brian

"Hold on, okay? I'm getting my weights out from under my bed."

"Sure."

It was Sunday afternoon, and I was on the phone with my girlfriend, Kristin Seltzer, for the second time that day. I knew it wasn't going to be the last time either. We've been having a lot of long phone conversations lately. Actually, they aren't really what you would call "conversations." We talk for a while and then just stay on the line, doing whatever we need to do, like homework, watching TV, or lifting pathetically small weights.

"Okay, I'm back," I said.

"Mrum brujt mejusnak," Kristin replied.

"What?"

"Sorry. My mom brought me some cheese and crackers," Kristin said. "Want to come over and help me eat them?"

"Can't," I said. "First I've got to do my weights workout so I can be big and buff when I grow

1

up, and then I have the famous Rainey family dinner, and then I have all my math homework to do. Wow—what a wild and crazy boyfriend you have!"

"And you have a pig for a girlfriend." Kristin giggled, chewing her snack noisily in my ear. "Hey, maybe you need to go on one of those talk shows my mom watches and get a life makeover."

"You're not a pig. You're hungry," I said. I started to do bicep curls with my free hand. Even though Kristin's weight is fine—she's healthy, not too skinny like a stick-thin supermodel—she still puts herself down sometimes. I don't know why she does it. She looks great to me.

"Yo! Brian!" my older brother, Billy, yelled up the stairs.

I put my hand over the receiver and poked my head out my bedroom door.

"I'm on the phone!" I yelled back.

"Well, get off," Billy called. "We're about to watch the game. You don't want to miss this, do you?" He and a couple of his friends were going to watch the final Lakers-Pacers game on tape before dinner. I'd been planning to bring my weights downstairs and work out while I watched.

"Oh, Brian, do you have to go?" I heard Kristin say. She sounded kind of sad.

2

I took my hand off the receiver. "Nah. Billy just asked me to watch a game with him. It's taped, though. I can watch it some other time," I told her.

"Oh, great!" Kristin said, sounding happy again. "Because I wanted to play you my new CatAttack CD. Have you heard it?"

"No, not yet." Actually, I hadn't even heard of the band. Every once in a while Kristin and her best friend, Lacey Frells, discover some girl band and go nuts over them. For about five minutes.

Still, I was curious. I'd just started playing in a band myself, so I'd been keeping an ear out for new sounds.

"All right, I'm pressing play. Can you hear it?" Kristin shouted into the phone.

I put down my weight so I could concentrate on listening. There was a noise like a vacuum cleaner, a ska drumbeat in the background, and a girl chanting, "I'd do anything. For you . . . *anything!* For you . . . *anything!* For you . . . *anything!*" in a gravelly voice.

I was pretty sure those lyrics were from a musical I'd seen with my family when I was little, although I couldn't remember which one it was. It seemed kind of twisted for CatAttack to be shouting those same lyrics and making them sound . . . well, *scary.*

3

"Hey, aren't those lyrics from *Annie* or *Oliver!* or something?" I asked.

"Isn't it great?" Kristin said, turning the music down. "Lacey and I are going to find out if they're touring soon and see if we can catch a show. Want to come?"

"Um. Sure," I said. What was I supposed to say? Seeing CatAttack play was definitely not at the top of my to-do list. But hey, Kristin's my girlfriend. And I'm a nice guy. I guess.

"Hey, Brian," my brother shouted upstairs again. "It's starting . . . !"

"That's okay. I'll watch it some other time," I shouted back. "Sorry about that," I said to Kristin. I lay down on the floor and put my feet up on my bed, getting comfortable. "So, what're you up to after school tomorrow?" I asked her.

But she wasn't there.

"Kristin?" No response. "Kristin?" I asked again.

There was a clicking noise. "Brian? Sorry— Lacey's on call waiting. Can I talk to you later?" Kristin said breathlessly. "Maybe we can do something tomorrow—like go for pizza after school, okay?"

"Um. Yeah. Okay," I said.

"Bye," Kristin said, and clicked off.

I pressed the off button on my portable

phone and lay there for a few seconds, just staring up at the ceiling. I should be psyched, right? I could just get up and go downstairs, and I would have missed only about five minutes of the game. But for some reason, I didn't feel like jumping up and going anywhere.

I felt like a flat tire.

Kristin

"So what are you going to wear tomorrow?" I asked my best friend, Lacey, after I'd hung up with Brian.

"I don't know," Lacey drawled. "Something boring, I guess. *All* of my clothes are boring."

It's weird. Lately Lacey and I have been reduced to talking about clothes. I don't think it will last long, but we actually don't have any major crises going on right now. All my school-activities stuff has quieted down for the time being. And Lacey just isn't the school-activities type of person. Stuff like that only gets in the way of her schedule.

"I bet Richard would like it if you wore your denim skirt and your black boots," I teased. Really, Richard Griggs would probably like Lacey in pretty much anything. They've had a crush on each other for ages, even though they're still not quite a "couple."

"I don't dress for anyone but myself," Lacey insisted. "And you shouldn't either. You don't hear me saying, 'Hey, Kristin, Brian loves you in that blue V-necked shirt,' do you?"

"No," I admitted.

Brian. Suddenly I felt bad about hanging up on him so quickly. But I was pretty sure he'd understand. We know each other so well. Besides, Brian hardly ever gets mad. He's too nice.

"But I'll tell you what *I* think you should wear," Lacey said. "I'm allowed to say because I'm your best friend and I'm not biased."

I laughed. "Oh, really?"

"I'm not biased—I just have good taste. And I think you should wear black sometimes," Lacey said.

"Black?" I repeated. I never wear black. Black is so . . . black. It doesn't do anything for me. It doesn't bring out my eyes or make me feel pretty, or happy, or anything like that. "Why should I wear black?" I asked.

"Because I said you should," Lacey answered simply.

"That's not a good enough reason," I argued.

"Okay, because Brian *told* me to tell you," Lacey said.

I giggled. As if. "He did not," I said.

"Yes, he did," Lacey replied.

"You're lying," I said, laughing again.

Lacey sighed. "Okay, I'm lying. Sweet little

Brian would never tell Krissy-Kris what to wear. It might hurt her feewings. But *I* still think you should try black. Think of the professional image you'll project at your student council meetings."

I knew Lacey was just kidding, but I hate it when she makes fun of Brian. "Okay," I relented. "If you promise not to say mean things about Brian, I promise to try wearing black. But not at school, at least not until I decide whether it's me or not."

"Cool," Lacey said. "How about tomorrow after school? We can go to that new Keanu Reeves movie at the mall. You can try on a few outfits before the movie starts."

"Deal," I agreed. What did I have to lose?

Sign on the Door of the Manchester Club

We like to hear our music *live!*
So if you've got a band
And you're any good,
Come play at our open mike.
It could be the beginning
of a beautiful friendship.
Who needs MTV
when they could have . . .
you!?
Saturday:
Show us what you've got.
To sign up, call Bette at 555-6738.

Brian

"Whatcha drawing?" I asked my friend Blue Spiccoli. It was Monday morning. We still had about ten minutes before the bell, and technically we didn't have to be in our seats until it rang. But Blue was already sitting down at his desk when I walked into the room. Which was a surprise since Blue is usually late for everything.

I peered over his shoulder at the piece of paper on his desk. "Is that for *Zone*?" I asked. Blue had recently joined the staff of the online magazine that I work on with a few other kids from our class. He had some great ideas, but he wasn't exactly an aspiring journalist. I was pretty sure the main reason he'd joined *Zone* was because Elizabeth Wakefield was on the staff too.

"Nah. I'm working on a design for our band poster, dude. Like it?" Blue put down his purple Magic Marker and held up the torn piece of loose-leaf he'd been scribbling on. I wasn't completely sure, but it looked like a volcano, some lightning, and a big wave, with the words *Big Noise!* written in capital letters at the bottom of the page. At least he'd spelled it right. One time we'd put an ad out for a girl bassist to join the band. No one even showed up to try out because Blue had written Big *Nose* on the ad. I mean, who would want to join a band with a name like that? It wasn't exactly an image-boosting experience.

Not that I was holding a grudge about it. Besides, it's not like we thought we were rock stars.

"What poster?" I asked, chuckling. "Oh, wait, I forgot. We're *touring,* right?" I laughed. I really crack myself up sometimes.

"Well, not *yet,* bro," Blue said, and put the drawing down. He was looking at me with the most intense expression I had ever seen on his face. Blue is the most laid-back guy I know, but he looked like he'd drunk a whole pot of espresso for breakfast.

"What do you mean, *yet?* What's up?" I asked.

Blue's blue eyes flew open, and he jumped up and grabbed my shoulders. "Listen, Bri. The Manchester Club is looking for new bands. They're having an open-mike gig next Saturday. All we gotta do is get a few songs together. You know, like a set, and we'll totally rock the house!" Blue waggled his eyebrows. "Are you with me, man? Can you dig it? They're going to love us!" he shouted. I'd never seen him like this. A couple of kids turned in their seats to stare at us.

"Us?" I repeated. I had absolutely no idea what he was talking about. "You mean Big Noise?"

"Yeah!" Blue grinned.

"At the Manchester Club?" I asked, dumbfounded. The Manchester Club is the coolest youth club in town. *Real* bands, like Splendora, play there. *Un*real bands, like ours, *don't* play there. We'd be laughed right off the stage. I cracked a smile. "You're kidding, right?"

"Absolutely not," Blue said, grinning like a lunatic.

"Forget it," I told him. "First of all, we only have two songs. Make that a song and a half. Second of all, we can't even play our one decent song without stopping in the middle because one of us has messed up. I mean, I can barely play the sax. How am I going to—and Salvador. Salvador is no—"

"Yo!"

Just before I could say something I might regret, Salvador loped over to us.

"Hey, Sal," Blue said. "Please explain to Brian that we are going to hit the Manchester Club and Sweet Valley like the Beatles hit England. First the Manchester Club, next stop, *the world!*"

Blue was shouting again. I wondered if maybe he'd worn earplugs the last time he'd gone surfing and had forgotten to take them out.

"Well, I wouldn't go that far," Salvador said. "But yeah, I was talking to Damon about it last night. I think it's worth a try." He moon-walked backward to his desk and did a little spin before sitting down in his chair. "I've been working on my moves."

Actually, he didn't look all that ridiculous. Salvador's got big feet, and he plays basketball like he's got ten of them—all lefties—but he's pretty graceful in his own way. And he's got rhythm. But his voice isn't exactly the greatest.

I turned back to Blue. "So you guys have all discussed this? How come I'm the last one to hear about it?"

"I tried to call you yesterday, but the phone was busy," Blue explained.

I felt my face heat up. Of course—I was talking on the phone to Kristin for most of the afternoon.

"So you guys are all set to play at the Manchester Club and I'm out because I don't have call waiting?" I asked, feeling kind of annoyed. More points for Rainey and his boring life. His best friends become famous while he sits in his room, talking to his girlfriend about . . . not much.

"No, man, you're in, you're in. Of course you're in!" Blue exclaimed.

That's one thing I love about Blue. His intentions are all good all the time. It's impossible to get mad at the guy.

"Come on, Bri. I'm telling you *now*," Blue continued. "You just saw how smooth our front man Salvador is. And you? You are the saxophone *king!* Damon has it all tied up with his funky guitar riffs"—he started drumming on the top of his desk—"and I've got the master beats. It's music, man. And it's time to make some noise!"

I tried to picture us up onstage at the Manchester Club. It was hard to even imagine it. But what I could imagine was seeing Kristin's face in the audience, looking up at me while I played her song.

Once she had a song, that is.

"All right," I said to Blue as I walked to my desk. "It's worth a shot. But we better practice."

"Yes!" Blue punched the air with his fist. "So—mandatory band practice every day, starting today after school. No excuses."

Today? But I was meeting Kristin today.

"Sorry, Blue, but I can't. I'm seeing Kristin. We haven't been hanging out that much since the

SVJH Olympics. I'm really sorry, but I promised."

Blue shook his head. "Dude," he said, frowning.

Salvador got up from his desk and walked over to us. "Come on, Brian. How are we going to get good if we don't practice? Kristin will understand. Just tell her you can't make it."

I thought about it, but it didn't feel right. I'd promised Kristin. That's all there was to it. That's why we had such a good relationship. We never let each other down. I wasn't about to start now.

"I can't. Sorry, guys," I said, looking down. "I promised. I can do it tomorrow, though."

Blue and Salvador looked at each other skeptically.

"Well, we already booked it with Damon," Blue said.

"Look, why don't you just practice without me?" I suggested. "I'll catch up, I promise."

Blue and Salvador looked at each other again.

"All right," Blue said reluctantly. "But don't let your girlfriend boss you around, okay? That's not cool."

I felt myself bristling. "I'm not!" I said.

Salvador patted my shoulder. "Take it easy, Brian. Blue just wants what's best for the band."

"That's right," Blue said. "We gotta stick together. We can't let girlfriends come between us.

15

Brian

Remember all that tension between the other Beatles and John because of Yoko?"

I had absolutely no clue what Blue was talking about. But I wasn't about to tell him that.

"Oh, absolutely," I said. "Don't worry—that'll never happen to us."

Salvador

"Gross." Anna Wang grimaced as she watched me mash potato chips into my tuna fish.

"Oh, and that's *not* gross?" I pointed to the place on her tray where Anna had written her name in butterscotch pudding.

We were sitting in the cafeteria at our usual table in the corner. Elizabeth Wakefield was sitting with us too, but she had run outside to look for her twin sister, Jessica, who was eating on the school steps with Damon Ross, her boyfriend and my band mate. Elizabeth had ended up with Jessica's lunch after Jessica had—apparently—spent an hour making her California roll last night, following the directions on the back of a package of gourmet seaweed. Elizabeth told us that Jessica had even forgone her usual Sunday-night pedicure to make sure the sushi was rolled just right. Elizabeth's plain old ham and cheese would be a major disappointment for her, and Elizabeth wouldn't dare

17

eat her twin's sushi. It's funny; their lunches were like perfect metaphors for them: Jessica is a California roll—she's got attitude, her looks are important to her, and she's difficult. Elizabeth is a ham sandwich—she's easy, down-to-earth, and always delicious. Okay, maybe that parallel doesn't quite work. And don't get me wrong; I like Jessica. I like sushi. But I'll take a ham sandwich any day.

"Finally," Elizabeth said, plunking her lunch bag on the table and pulling up a chair. "I'm starving." She opened up the bag and tore into her sandwich.

I smiled at her. Even when Elizabeth is stuffing her face, she looks like an angel. The cafeteria is air-conditioned, but her shoulder-length blond hair was radiating this golden warmth.

"So, Jessica and Damon were talking about Big Noise playing at the Manchester Club. Is that true?" Elizabeth asked, her blue-green eyes fixed on me, curious. I probably had mayonnaise on the end of my nose, but it would be just like Elizabeth not to even notice. I swiped at my face with my napkin anyway and cleared my throat.

"Yeah. We're playing at their open mike next Saturday. And if they like us, I guess they might give us some regular gigs," I explained. My palms started sweating. Just thinking about playing at the Manchester Club was making me very nervous.

"Wow," Anna said, sounding impressed. "Will you still hang out with us when you're all famous?"

Elizabeth giggled and waved the piece of waxed paper her sandwich had been wrapped in at me. "Can I have your autograph?" she asked, like an overzealous groupie.

I folded my arms across my chest. "Well, I don't exactly think we're going to rocket to stardom," I said modestly. "But we are getting better."

Anna looked at her watch. "Oops. Sorry, guys," she said, standing up. "I promised Larissa I'd help her study for Spanish. She's got twenty adjectives to memorize before the bell rings."

"Want to come over to my house later?" Elizabeth asked her.

Anna shook her head and shrugged. "I've got to rehearse a scene with Toby. But I'll call you guys tonight, okay?"

Elizabeth and I nodded, and Anna turned to go.

"Later, Anna," I called, and took a huge bite of my sandwich.

"So what songs are you going to play?" Elizabeth asked. She knew as well as I did that the Big Noise song repertoire could be counted on two fingers.

Salvador

"Well, we're going to have to come up with some new ones," I admitted. "Any ideas?" Elizabeth is an excellent writer, so I figured I might milk her creative talent.

"How about a song called 'Can I Have a Bite of Your Sandwich?' It could be about someone who wants to try something new without giving up her own . . . um . . . sandwich." Elizabeth looked at me hungrily.

Actually she was looking at my *sandwich* hungrily. I held it out to her. She blushed and took a little bite off the corner.

"Good?" I asked her.

Elizabeth smacked her lips and cocked her head thoughtfully. "Interesting," she said. "I wonder what it would taste like if you used barbecue potato chips instead of plain."

"Nasty," I said.

"Hey, that's a cool name for a song—'Nasty,'" Elizabeth suggested.

"I think Janet Jackson took care of that one," I said, laughing.

"Good point," she replied. "Hmmm." Elizabeth stroked her chin thoughtfully.

"But maybe this will inspire you," I said. I picked up my Oreo cookies and covered my eyes with them.

"'Oreo Eyes'!" Elizabeth crowed.

20

I put down the cookies and grabbed a banana. "Ooh, baby, I love your big, brown Oreo eyes . . . ," I sang, holding my banana up like a microphone.

Elizabeth clutched her hands to her heart like I was this breathtaking rock god that she completely idolized.

I wish.

Wait a minute. No, I don't.

Elizabeth and I are friends. Pals. Comrades. Compadres. Nothing more. And I'm happy with that. We both are. At least, I think she is.

And I think I am.

I think.

Kristin

"Here," I said, putting my brownie on Brian's tray. "I'll trade you." I reached for his butterscotch pudding. Brian grabbed my wrist and snapped at my hand like a rabid dog.

"Grrr!" he growled. "Hands off my pudding!"

"I thought you hated pudding," I said, taking back my brownie.

Brian shrugged. "I'm a musician. I'm artistic. I'm fickle," he said. He took a spoonful of pudding and made a face.

I took a bite of my brownie. "*Mmmm.* This is the *best* brownie I have ever eaten," I said in an exaggerated voice. "I can't believe you didn't want any. Lucky me, I get to eat the *whole* thing. *Yum!*"

Brian swiped the brownie out of my hand and took a huge bite before I could stop him. "Brian!" I whined.

It took a minute for him to finish swallowing it. "So," he said when he was done. "You want to get pizza later? Or we could rent a movie."

I stared at the bowl of pudding on his tray. "Oh, sorry, Brian. I told Lacey I'd go to the mall with her after school." I looked up at him. "You don't mind, do you?" I asked.

Brian frowned. "I thought we made plans," he said. Was I imagining things, or did he look seriously upset?

I shrugged. "We can hang out tomorrow."

"You said *today*." Brian's eyes were getting darker, I swear. "I thought we had a date," he said. "I even told the guys I couldn't practice after school today because you and I had plans."

"You did?" I asked, genuinely surprised. *I have the best boyfriend in the whole world,* I thought. Only Brian would say no to the guys in his band so he could spend time with me. "Oh, Brian, you're so nice. Sometimes I wonder if I deserve you. It's like you're *too* nice."

Uh-oh. Brian's eyes were almost black now. In fact, his whole face looked like a thundercloud. I decided I'd better backpedal.

"I'm sorry, Brian, but Lacey already told Victoria she can't watch her little sister until we get back from the mall," I explained. "But I could call and see if she can do it tomorrow," I added hastily.

"Don't bother," Brian said. He pushed back his chair and stood up. "Too nice, huh?" he huffed. "Maybe you're right." Then without another word he stalked over to the big orange garbage can in the corner, dumped his tray (pudding and all), and stormed out of the cafeteria.

I had definitely said the wrong thing. But what's wrong with telling someone he's *nice*?

Brian

Ping.

I threw a rock at our tin mailbox and took the steps up to my house three at a time. I had come straight home after school. No way could I face the guys at band practice after I had made such a big deal about having to spend quality time with Kristin. Even if I did need the practice. And believe me, we *all* needed it. That is, if we weren't going to completely embarrass ourselves next Saturday, which we were going to do anyway because we stunk, and the only reason no one would admit it was that—as Kristin would say—we were all *too nice*.

I slammed the front door, tossed my backpack into the corner of the kitchen, and hurled myself at the refrigerator. No more whole milk. As usual, my selfish older brother had hogged all the milk that morning, and now the only thing left for me to drink was skim. I picked up the carton. It was only about a third full. If I had a glass, then Ellie wouldn't have enough for her banana smoothie, which she always has when she gets back from her dance class on Mondays. I put the carton back. I guess *nice* guys drink water.

"Oh, thank goodness you're here, Brian," my mother said, rushing into the kitchen. She was wearing her tennis outfit. "Sam and I have our tennis lessons in five minutes. Billy said he'd watch Addie until we get back, but in his usual thoughtful way, he seems to have forgotten. Ellie's at dance. Would you mind looking after your sister until your father gets home?"

I stared at my boring glass of water. Everyone else in my family had such hectic, exciting lives. I was the only one who had nothing to do but stay home and watch cartoons with my eight-year-old sister while drinking a refreshing glass of water. Wowee.

"Fine," I said.

My mother reached out and cupped her hand under my chin. "I don't know what I did to deserve such a wonderful son," she said, looking at me adoringly. Then she whirled around and snatched up the car keys. "Sam! Let's go!" she yelled up the stairs. "See you in a few!" she called out to me, and dashed out the door.

Sam, my twelve-year-old sister, came barreling down the stairs with her tennis racket. "Hi,

Brian. Bye, Brian!" she yelled, flying out the door after my mother.

I took a sip of water. It tasted like water.

"Brian?" I heard Addie call from the living room. "Will you make me a snack?"

"What do you want?" I called back.

"I want toast, but I want you to cut holes in the middle of it and cut the crusts off. And can I have jelly on it?"

I sighed. Lately Addie has been in this phase where she's incredibly particular about her food. My mother makes a point of always making exactly what she wants because she thinks Addie must be craving things her body needed to grow. I'm not so sure. I mean, toast with a hole in the middle and no crust has to have fewer vitamins than normal toast, right?

"Just a minute," I called. I got out the bread and took out a slice. I cut a hole out of the middle of it and ate the little circle of bread. So my afternoon snack consisted of a glass of water and a morsel of bread. What was this, prison?

"Don't cut the hole too big," Addie warned from the living room. I looked down at the slice of bread. Was the hole too big? Maybe a little. I took out another slice and cut a smaller hole, eating that one too. Then I decided that one was

27

too big too, so I took out a third slice and cut another hole.

Just then my brother, Billy, walked through the front door.

"Hey," he said, striding into the kitchen. He opening the refrigerator, picked up the skim milk, and drank the whole thing down, just like that, right out of the carton.

"Ahhh," he said. Then he burped. "Whatcha makin'?" he asked me.

"Addie's toast," I said. I looked at him expectantly, waiting for him to apologize for coming home late when he was supposed to be baby-sitting Addie. I was waiting for him to take over the toast making so I could get on with my life. Maybe when I was done finishing my glass of water, I could do something really thrilling like lie on my bed and stare at the ceiling.

"Cool," Billy said. He turned around and headed for the stairs.

That's when I lost it.

"Billy!" I yelled. "Did it ever occur to you that I have a life too? It's your turn to watch Addie, remember? I love the way you all just assume that I have nothing better to do than poke holes in toast all day. Maybe the *old* Brian would have been happy with that. But not anymore. The *old* Brian was nice. Too nice. The new Brian doesn't poke holes in toast. The new Brian doesn't drink water." I tossed my water into the sink, pulled open the refrigerator, and grabbed the first bottle I saw. I took a swig. It was lemon juice. I spat it out, rinsed my mouth out with water, and then spat that out too. Billy was staring at me like I was insane.

"The new Brian doesn't let people walk all over him," I continued. I grabbed the jar of jelly and tossed it at Billy. He caught it, still staring at me with wide eyes. "Addie wants toast with holes and jelly and no crusts," I said. "Get to it." Then I stormed out of the house.

I was going to band practice no matter what. And if the guys teased me about Kristin, they were going to be sorry.

Salvador

"Don't step on her shoes 'cause Granny proves—she can cha-cha!" I sang into the microphone.

Big Noise was just finishing up our first song. We were missing Brian's sax, but we sounded okay.

Just then Brian strode into Blue's garage. He didn't even say "hey." He just picked up his sax, put the strap around his neck, licked his lips, and started playing. Loud.

Wooot. Honk. Wooot. Bleeehht.

I put my hands over my ears. Brian was like a man possessed. He wouldn't stop.

Blue and Damon stopped playing. We exchanged concerned glances.

"Let's take five, guys," Blue shouted over the ruckus. But Brian kept right on playing. "Easy, Bri, you might break a window, man." Blue chuckled, but Brian wasn't amused. In fact, he didn't seem to have heard what Blue said. His eyes were closed, his face was beet red, and he was putting everything he had into making the scariest sounds I've ever heard.

Hoonkkaaawaahhnnk.

Someone had to put a stop to this. I grabbed the mike. "Brian. Earth to Brian. Please put down your saxophone and put your hands above your head. It's for your own good, Brian. Put down the sax."

Brian opened his eyes and stopped playing.

"What?" he said, looking bewildered. "What's the matter?"

"Oh, nothing," Damon said, pretending to tune his guitar. "We really enjoyed your solo. Is that a new song?"

"Brian, what are you doing here anyway?" Blue asked. "I thought you couldn't make it."

"Yeah, well, my plans changed," Brian said, looking annoyed.

"Kristin ditch you or something?" I teased.

Okay. Normally Brian is like this soft, sweet marshmallow of a guy that never even raises an eyebrow with any hint of negativity. But that Brian must have been abducted by aliens because this Brian was shooting lasers at me and smoke was practically coming out of his nostrils.

"What did you say?" he demanded.

"Um." I gulped, glancing at Blue and Damon for backup.

31

"Hey, what's got into you, dude?" Blue asked. Brian shot him the same look of death. The thing with Blue is, no one can be mad at him. He's just too . . . Blue. "Yo, Bri. We're your mates, mate. That's what the band's about, man. It's cool. You can talk to us," Blue said in his best groovy English accent, like he was the newest member of the Beatles circa 1965.

Brian looked unsure. Then he took a deep breath. "Kristin said I was too nice," he explained.

There was a moment of silence. Then we all nodded in understanding. At least *I* understood. It was practically the story of my life. You don't wind up with more girl friends than guy friends and no girlfriends at all by being un-nice. But being called too nice was the kiss of death. A too nice guy is the kind of guy you can treat like dirt and who will still come back for more. Pathetic. Calling a guy too nice is like spraying him with vanishing liquid. It means automatic invisibility. It is very uncool.

"That's not right," Damon said.

"That is so wrong," Blue agreed.

"That's the worst," I said.

Brian nodded. "I'm too nice, and everyone says they don't deserve me, but they still walk all over me and don't think for a minute that I mind," he said.

We all nodded.

"And I've had it. My nice days are over," Brian said.

Damon started plucking out a few notes on his guitar.

Blue tapped his snare drum and clanked his cymbals a couple of times.

"Mnnn," I hummed into the mike, picking up the rhythm. "You say I'm too nice, but I disagree . . . ," I started to sing. "Let me give you some advice—don't you mess with me."

Brian nodded and blew a few tentative notes into his sax.

"All this nice may be nice for you, but it's not nice for me!"

We kept it up for a few more bars, and I kept improvising the lyrics.

Wait a minute. Something was clicking here. We sounded *good*.

I couldn't believe it. Suddenly it felt like everything was coming together. We had a new song, and it seriously rocked. All we'd needed was a little rage!

Brian

"Thank you, ladies and gentlemen!" Salvador said into the mike in his best rock-star voice after we'd finished playing "Too Nice" for the fifth time. "You're all invited to party with us in our suite afterward. Oh yes! Calm down, girls. I know, I'm irresistible!"

I shook my head. What a goofball.

"Hey, why don't we invite the girls to come hear us practice tomorrow?" Blue suggested. "See what they think of our new tune. Besides, we gotta get used to playing in front of an audience. It's a whole different scene playing to a sea of faces, not just that old piece of junk." He pointed to the old, rusty lawn mower parked permanently in the corner of his garage.

"I'll call Jessica and see if she wants to come," Damon offered.

"And I'll call Anna and Elizabeth," Salvador offered.

They looked at me.

The thing was, I really didn't want Kristin to

hear "Too Nice." It was clearly our best song. But it was also so clearly about what Kristin had said to me. There was no way she could hear the words to the song and not feel hurt by them.

"I don't know, guys," I said. "I mean, that was good—like spontaneous improvisation—but don't you think we could change the words? It would still be the same song; we could just . . . you know, soften it up a bit."

They stared at me.

"Soften it up?" Blue asked, incredulous.

"All great songs come out of a spontaneous moment. Never mess around with the creative impulse," Damon said.

"It's about time we got in touch with our bad selves anyway," Salvador said. "We were looking like a goody-goody boy band before. Now we've got . . . bad-boy appeal." He had a smug look on his face, like he was really pleased for thinking up the bad-boy thing.

I still wasn't convinced.

"The song isn't about Kristin anyway," Blue said. "It's about every guy who's ever been told by any girl that he's too nice. That's what makes it so brilliant, man. It's universal." Blue made a big, swooping gesture over his head with his drumsticks.

I still didn't think Kristin would see it that way.

35

"And see, this is exactly what we're talking about in the song," Salvador added. "You've got to start thinking of *yourself* sometimes, man."

"So what do you want to do, Brian?" Damon asked.

All three guys were looking at me expectantly, challenging me.

What did I want? I thought about it.

I didn't want to hurt Kristin, but I didn't want to be the kind of guy that people barely notice because they're just so . . . nice.

This was my chance to turn things around. And it wasn't like we were doing anything wrong. "Too Nice" totally rocked, and everyone else, besides Kristin, would be totally into it.

"All right, let's leave the song like it is," I agreed, trying to sound confident and cool about it.

I'd just have to make sure that Kristin never heard it.

"Too Nice"

You say I'm too nice,
But I disagree.
Let me give you some advice—
Don't you mess with me.
All this nice may be nice for you,
But it's not nice for me.

Chorus:
I'm taking back my CDs,
Eatin' pizza, extra cheese,
I'm playing games with the boys;
We're makin' lots of *big noise!*

You said I was cute,
You said I was fly,
But I've got somethin' to tell you,
And it starts with, "Bye-bye!"

Second chorus:
Say good-bye to Mr. Nice,
Yeah, he's hittin' the road.
Find some other guy to step on
'Cause I'm in a new mode.
Don't think twice; Mr. Nice
Was nice, but he isn't me.

Kristin

"What about this?" Lacey asked, giggling. She held up a black, glittery halter top. It didn't even have a back, just strings.

I rolled my eyes. "I don't think so," I said.

We were in Fashion Train, Lacey's favorite store at the mall. We had an hour to kill before the movie, which gave me a chance to try on a few black outfits and see how they felt.

I fingered a sleeveless black turtleneck sweater. It was cool, not at all revealing, and kind of mature. I held it up to myself and looked in the mirror. Not bad. It was a maybe. I studied my face in the mirror. I looked weird, kind of tired and worried. And I knew why. Ever since lunch I had been worrying about Brian and me.

"Would you like to try that on, miss?" the saleswoman asked me. I blushed. I knew she was only trying to be helpful, but it's embarrassing finding out that someone's been watching you look at yourself in the mirror.

"Go on, Kristin," Lacey said.

"All right," I relented.

The woman held back the red velvet curtain to the dressing room in the corner of the store. I went inside, carrying the sweater, and she let the curtain fall.

"Let me know if you need another size or if you'd like to try anything else," she said, and then I heard her walk away.

I took off my pale blue T-shirt and pulled the black turtleneck sweater over my head, tugging it down over the waistband of my jeans. I pulled my hair out from where it had gotten stuck inside the high collar. Then I examined myself.

The sweater fit perfectly. It wasn't too tight or too loose. It wasn't too short, so my belly button showed, or too long, so that it bulked up on my hips. It felt nice and soft and seemed to be made well. I looked good in it too—older, serious, and sort of sexy.

It totally wasn't me.

I changed back into my T-shirt and stepped out of the dressing room. Lacey looked at me expectantly from across the store.

"So?" she asked.

"Maybe in a different color," I said.

"Typical." Lacey sighed and tossed me the same sweater in lavender.

I took it back to the dressing room to try on.

Kristin

I stared at myself in the mirror.

I still didn't like the way I looked, but it wasn't because of the sweater. The sweater was very me, and the color suited me perfectly. It was my face that was ruining the picture. That worried look still hadn't gone away.

I had to talk to Brian.

Elizabeth

"Of course I would," I heard Jessica tell Damon. "Why don't you bring your sisters with you to Blue's house, and we can all watch you play?"

Wow. My twin has really changed over the past few months. Having a boyfriend as sweet and generous as Damon has really brought out the best in her. Not that she was ever a bad person . . . she's just better than ever these days.

It was Monday night, and I'd already done all my homework. Now I was sitting in front of the computer we share, trying to come up with a new article for *Zone,* the online magazine I started with Anna and Salvador. The cursor was blinking on the empty screen, but I couldn't think of anything I wanted to write. I examined my cuticles. *Maybe I should ask Jessica to do my nails,* I thought. Through the bathroom that separates our rooms I could see Jessica lying on her bed, with her feet dangling over the end. Her toenails were painted bright yellow.

I looked at the computer's blank screen again. I wanted to write something funny, but I wasn't feeling funny. Salvador was funny. No matter what mood he was in, he could make you laugh. Blue was funny, but in a different way. He was more outrageous because he lived so differently from most of the people I knew. His parents died a long time ago, so he just lived with his older brother, Leaf. Salvador didn't live with his parents either, but the Doña, his grandmother, seemed like a pretty good substitute. In fact, she's just about the coolest grandmother anyone could wish for.

"Liz? Anyone home?"

Jessica was standing in my bedroom doorway, holding out the phone, which she'd dragged on its long cord across the bathroom floor. "It's Blue, for you. I hung up with Damon just so you guys could talk." She waved the receiver at me, teasing. "I know what he's going to ask you."

"Give me that!" I snatched the phone out of her hand. "Hello? Blue?" I said.

"Hey, Elizabeth. How's it going?"

"I'm trying to write something for *Zone,* but my mind keeps wandering."

"I know how you feel," Blue said. "I have that problem all the time. Except when I'm surfing. That's the only time I'm really focused."

Blue is really into surfing. He even taught me how so I could write an article about it for *Zone*. But when I surf, I definitely don't feel focused. I feel like a major spaz!

"So, I was wondering if maybe you wanted to come hear the band practice tomorrow after school. We have a new song that's actually pretty groovy. And if you had time, we could hang out afterward too," Blue said.

"Sure," I replied. "That would be fun."

"Jessica said she was going, and I think Salvador said he'd invite Anna, and Brian will probably invite Kristin. So there will be a bunch of us. It'll be cool," Blue said.

"That'll be great," I agreed.

"Rad. Okay, then, see you tomorrow," Blue said.

"See you." I hung up.

At first I couldn't really imagine Blue, Salvador, Damon, and Brian forming a band together or even being friends—they're just so different. It would be like Jessica, Anna, Kristin, and me forming an all-girl punk band. Just the thought made me smile.

Elizabeth

"Isn't it the coolest?" Jessica said, bounding into my room and bouncing on my bed, knocking over a pile of clean, folded laundry.

"What?" I asked, swiveling in my desk chair to face her.

"That our boyfriends play in the same band," Jessica shot back.

I narrowed my eyes at her. "Blue is not my boyfriend," I said indignantly. "We're friends. That's all."

Jessica rolled her eyes. "Okay, well, what about El Salvador, then?"

"Same thing," I insisted. "We're just friends—you know that, Jess."

"Okay, fine. I'll buy that. But come on, Liz. Why don't you just admit that you like Blue?"

I shook my head at her. "You know, it *is* possible to have a friend that just so happens to be a boy. He doesn't have to be your boyfriend."

"Okay, okay," Jessica said. "But tell me it's not a tiny bit flattering to be asked by a friend who just so happens to be a boy to watch his band play in his garage?"

Just then our phone rang again. I picked it up on the first ring, hoping Jessica would get the hint and leave me alone.

"Hello?"

"Hey."

It was Salvador.

"Oh, hi, Salvador," I said. "What's up?"

"Well, I wanted to ask if you have time after school tomorrow to maybe come and watch the band practice. It's at Blue's house."

"Yeah, I know. Blue just called me," I told him. "I said I'd come."

"Blue called you?" Salvador asked. He sounded surprised. I don't know why, though. Blue and I are just friends—Salvador knows that.

"He said you guys have a great new song. You didn't actually persuade them to play 'Oreo Eyes,' did you?" I asked, laughing.

"I'm planning to," Salvador said. "But not yet. Anyway, wait till you hear this new one— it rocks."

"I can't wait," I said. I caught Jessica's eye. She was examining her eyebrows in the bathroom mirror, and just then she raised them very pointedly at me.

"Well, see you tomorrow," Salvador said.

"Bye," I said, and hung up.

Now Jessica was wiggling her eyebrows at me in a ridiculously suggestive way.

I ignored her and swiveled my chair back

45

Elizabeth

to face the blank computer screen and its annoying flashing cursor. I still couldn't think of anything to write. I was too busy thinking how nice it felt to be asked by two friends who just happened to be boys to go hear their band practice.

Brian

"Geek," I whispered.

I turned away from the mirror and opened the bottom drawer of my dresser, searching for a less hopeless T-shirt or a more inspiring pair of pants. Nothing. How could I go to school looking like this? It was so embarrassing.

Not that anything had changed overnight. My nose hadn't grown a foot, and I hadn't shaved off my eyebrows in a bout of momentary insanity. But that was exactly the point. I looked the same way I always did. Except now, when I looked in the mirror, I felt like I might as well have *nice* written in puffy, round, girlie writing on my forehead. With a heart dotting the *i*.

It was disgusting.

"Billy?" I called, poking my head out my bedroom door.

"I'm in here," Billy yelled from the bathroom. He takes longer in the bathroom than me and my sisters combined. "What do you want?"

47

"Can I borrow some of your clothes?" I yelled back. "Mine are all . . . dirty."

Billy opened the bathroom door. He had shaving cream on one side of his face and a towel around his waist. He looked very mature. Just the look I was going for. But I couldn't exactly go to school wearing shaving cream.

"What's wrong with those clothes?" Billy asked, looking me up and down.

"These?" I said, glaring down at my khaki pants and green polo shirt. "They're too . . ." I fumbled for a good answer. "Boring."

Billy cocked his head and—for once—didn't make a wisecrack. "Knock yourself out," he said, starting to close the bathroom door. "Just don't spill anything on them, okay?"

"Thanks," I said, and made a beeline for his room.

Billy likes the baggy-pants-and-oversized-football-shirt look. Most of his pants are frayed at the hems because they're so long, and he steps on them. I found a cool black-and-yellow football jersey with the number nine on it and a great pair of black combat pants. I had to roll them up and wear a belt, but when I checked myself out in the mirror, the result was more than satisfying. I slouched against the wall and admired the guy slouching against the wall in the mirror. He certainly didn't look nice. He looked handsome and dangerous. At least, I hoped Kristin would think so.

Establishing a new image first thing in the morning takes time. I was running late. I flew down the stairs, bumping into my big sister, Ellie, who was shuffling out of the kitchen, clutching a glass of orange juice.

"What's that for?" Ellie asked.

"What?" I said, scrambling around for my backpack.

"Your outfit." She yawned, pointing at me.

"What's wrong with it?" I asked.

Ellie studied me for a moment. Then she smiled and took a sip of her juice. "Oh, nothing," she said.

On the way to school I forgot about my clothes and thought about what I was going to say to Kristin. I felt bad for storming off in the middle of lunch yesterday without any real explanation. Today I was going to apologize and then ask her to come to band practice. I was even going to tell her about our song, "Too Nice," just to kind of warn her. Then, I was hoping, if she heard it with the other girls there and they liked it, she wouldn't be too upset.

"Hey, number nine," I heard Kristin's voice

call out on the way to my locker. "What's with the droopy drawers?"

I whirled around to see Kristin smiling at me. She was wearing a light purple sleeveless sweater I hadn't seen before. She looked really pretty.

"Hey," I said, walking up to her.

"How come you're wearing Billy's clothes?" she asked. "Did you run out of clean laundry or something?"

For some reason, it really bugged me that it didn't even occur to her that I might come to school in a cool outfit because I *wanted* to. "No, did *you?*" I snapped. Suddenly I didn't feel like asking her to come to band practice to hear "Too Nice." Suddenly I didn't feel very nice at all.

We just stood there facing each other for a second. I think Kristin was holding her breath. I avoided her eyes, staring down at my rolled-up pants legs. Then I turned around and walked quickly to my locker, leaving her staring after me.

I felt bad, but it felt good to be bad.

Sort of.

Kristin

Hello?

I just stood there, watching Brian stomp off in that oversized football/military outfit.

What. Is. The. Deal? I thought. *What happened to my sweet boyfriend? Where did this jerk come from?*

The second bell rang, and kids were rushing past me on all sides to get to their classrooms. I hitched my backpack onto my shoulder and started walking to algebra. Two golden blond heads bobbed past me.

"See you at band practice, Kristin," Elizabeth Wakefield called over her shoulder. Jessica whirled around, walking backward to her class. She was wearing a long, pink tube skirt and had to take little tiny steps, like a geisha.

"Hey, Kristin. I'm going to the guys' practice too. Let's all walk over to Blue's right after history, okay?" Jessica suggested.

I nodded, and the twins rushed off to their classes.

Kristin

Suddenly I didn't care if I made it to class or not. *Hello?*

So everyone had been invited to watch the guys' band practice. Everyone, that is, except me. Could that be because the person who was supposed to invite me had barely said two words to me in the past two days? I hugged myself and bit my quivering lower lip. Was Brian breaking up with me?

I spun on my heel and headed for the girls' room. Lacey was on her way out. I could tell she'd been in there primping. Her lips were all glittery with a new coat of gloss, and her dark brown hair was freshly brushed.

"Hey, what are *you* doing wandering the halls after the second bell, Madam President of the Eighth Grade?" Lacey scolded, her hands on her hips. "That's usually my area of expertise." Then I guess she noticed how upset I was because her face fell, and she looked a little worried.

I shrugged, and Lacey followed me into the bathroom. I blew my nose, washed my hands, and wiped invisible smudged mascara from my eyes.

"Want to borrow my Sticky Toffee Lip Candy?" Lacey asked. Lacey has this way of dealing with me when I'm upset about something that might seem kind of insensitive but that I really appreciate sometimes. She just doesn't mention it.

I took the tube of lip stuff from her and started smearing my lips with it. It smelled like caramel, and my stomach growled noisily.

"Did you see what Brian is wearing today?" Lacey asked. "He's in a band, so now he's, like, a gangsta rapper or something? Next thing you know, he'll shave his head and bleach it blond."

I pressed my lips together and twisted the lip-gloss top back on. I was about to say something in Brian's defense, but then I stopped myself.

"Uh-huh," was all I said. "Can I borrow your brush?"

Lacey handed me the brush. "Here. Better hurry, though, or we'll both get detention. Hey, what are you doing later?"

I yanked at my hair with the brush, hard. Me? After school? I was doing nothing. Absolutely nothing at all. Because my boyfriend, who I normally would have been doing something with, was having band practice, which, for no reason at all, I was not invited to. What were they practicing so much all of a sudden anyway?

"Because I was hoping," Lacey went on, "that maybe you could come to the Cue Café with me and Richard and my cousin, Trent. He and my uncle Tomás are staying with us for a week.

Kristin

Tomás is Victoria's brother, so you can guess what he's like, but Trent is the coolest. He's fifteen, and *so cute*. You'd totally like him. Wanna come?"

It wasn't like I had anything better to do. Playing a good game of pool might take my mind off the fact that Brian had just randomly decided to be mean to me. Especially if it was a game of pool with Lacey's cute older cousin.

"Sure," I said, and handed Lacey back her brush.

"Good." Lacey grabbed my arm and pulled me out of the bathroom. "Now, come on, you big troublemaker, you," she said sarcastically. "Time to go to class."

We ran, laughing all the way down the hall and screeching past a glaring Mr. Wilfred on our way into class.

I felt so much better. I told you Lacey has a way with me.

Note Passed to Jessica Wakefield from Kristin Seltzer in Last Period, Mr. Harriman's History Class

Hey, Jessica,
Gotta love Marie Antoinette's sense of style, even if she did get beheaded. Anyway, I can't go to hear Big Noise practice with you guys. I totally forgot, but Lacey's cousin Trent is visiting, and I promised her I'd hang with them and Richard Griggs at Cue Café.
Have fun, though. Byeee!
— Kristin

Hey, Kristin,
No biggie. Have a good time. I'll call you later.
Love,
Jessica

Elizabeth

"All this nice may be nice for you!"

Wackawacka.

"But it's not nice for me!"

Badoom dop.

"Whoa, whoa, baby . . ." Salvador was singing with his eyes closed, his face all twisted in mock rage. He was wearing this nice dark blue polo shirt and kept making these cute arm gestures while he sang. He definitely had rock-star charisma.

Blue was banging away on the drums, keeping the beat and smiling like a bright sun at the back of the room.

Brian had his back to us and was playing the sax in a kind of conversation with what Damon was playing on his guitar. Like a call-and-response sort of thing. It sounded really cool.

I have to say, I was impressed. I glanced over at my sister to see if she was as into them as I was. That would be a yes. Jessica was bobbing her head like crazy and bouncing around in her chair, her eyes glued to Damon. Next to her, Damon's adorable little sisters, Kaia and Sally, were squealing and dancing and singing along.

I never thought I'd say this, but Big Noise was actually really good.

> *"Say good-bye to Mr. Nice,*
> *Yeah, he's hittin' the road.*
> *Find some other guy to step on*
> *'Cause I'm in a new mode.*
> *Don't think twice; Mr. Nice*
> *Was nice, but he isn't me."*

The song ended in a frenzy of Blue's cymbals and Salvador's vicious lyrics. Salvador did a little spin and then threw himself down on the ground, rolling around like he was in pain.

"Ahhh! It hurts! It hurts! We are so good, it hurts me!" he cried. He's such a clown.

"So, what'd you think?"

I looked up, and Blue was staring down at me anxiously, a drumstick tucked behind each ear. They looked like antlers.

"I loved it!" I answered honestly. "You guys sound great. Really professional."

Elizabeth

"Awesome," Blue said, his eyes shining happily. He held up his hand, and we high-fived. He smiled at me, and I felt it all the way down to my toes.

He has such beautiful blue eyes.

Salvador

What just happened? Was it just me, or were Elizabeth and Blue, like, *holding hands?* Okay, maybe not exactly. But close enough. I was about to yell, "Hands off, man!" But I thought that might be going a bit too far.

"Hey, Salvador," Elizabeth called over to me while I was still writhing around on the floor, getting in touch with my inner Mick Jagger. "I knew you could do happy, and I knew you could do silly, but I had no idea you could do angst. You really sang that song like you meant it."

"Yeah, well. I've been there, I guess," I said. I rested my chin in my hands and studied Elizabeth's face. She wasn't blushing or anything. I wished she was. I wished Elizabeth Wakefield got at least a little self-conscious or squirmy or itchy or *something* when she talked to me instead of looking like she could have been talking to Jessica, or her brother, Steven, or . . . a chair. I guess I really did suffer from the too nice disease. I mean, why couldn't I make people uncomfortable every once in a while?

"Uh, Elizabeth, I was wondering . . . ," Blue said, tapping Elizabeth on the shoulder. I sat up and pretended to examine my thumbnail. "So," he said to Elizabeth, "do you want to check out my new RipTide game?"

"Sure!" Elizabeth said, like that was the best proposition she'd ever heard. "But don't expect me to be good. You've seen me on a surfboard."

"No way—don't put yourself down like that. You're awesome," Blue said.

Even my fascinating thumb cuticle couldn't distract me from what was obviously happening here. I saw it with my own eyes. *They were both blushing.*

Humph. Was something going on here that I should know about? I mean, they were friends; I knew that. They were on the volleyball team together, and Blue taught Elizabeth to surf. But I didn't know anything had *developed* between them. And if Elizabeth liked Blue, then why hadn't I heard about it? I was supposed to be one of her best friends. And if Blue liked Elizabeth, then why hadn't he asked me any man-to-man questions about her? I mean, were they just so sure of themselves that they didn't even need me?

Now I was the one getting uncomfortable.

I glanced at the other side of the room, where

Brian was carrying Damon's older sister on his shoulders and Damon was holding the littler one upside down by her feet while Jessica tickled her. Jessica looked up for a second at Blue and Elizabeth, then looked at me and winked. I have absolutely no idea why—Jessica isn't a winker. She's more of a stick-out-her-tonguer. But it was definitely a wink.

"Come on, Jess," Damon said. "We've got to get these girls home to eat their snakes and eels."

"Eeew!" Kaia and Sally screamed.

"I'll head out with you guys," Brian said. "I was thinking about getting a haircut on the way home."

I guess Brian had decided to revamp his look now that he was a rock god. I noticed he had on some new duds too. *Well, at least he's into it now,* I thought.

"Hey, Salvador," Elizabeth called. "Want to stay and play video games with me and Blue?"

Humph again. I could have said yes so I could keep my eye on them. See if my suspicions were valid. But what if they were only trying to be nice and they really didn't want me there? How embarrassing. Better to show them I really didn't care.

"No thanks," I said. "I've got to get home and help the Doña . . . wash . . . um . . . mushrooms.

61

Salvador

Yes, tonight is her mushroom-picking night. There are bound to be barrels full of them, and they all need washing," I chirped pleasantly.

See? I really didn't care. Not one little bit.

Oh, shut up! I thought.

I think I might be losing my mind.

Kristin

"Yellow ball, center pocket," Lacey said, biting her lip. She took a wide stance and leveled the stick in between her thumb and forefinger and lined up the shot. I bent down to see how difficult it was going to be.

"Not a chance," Richard whispered. "She's holding the stick all wrong for that shot."

Lacey's head whipped around, and she glared at him. Then she turned back to the cue ball and made the shot. *Whap!* The yellow ball dropped right into the center pocket.

Lacey lifted her arms over her head. "I'd like to thank my trainer and all my fans," she said, looking out, misty-eyed, at an imaginary crowd, like some Olympic athlete who had just won the gold. The Cue Café was pretty crowded, and nobody was paying any attention to us, so it wasn't as embarrassing as it sounds.

Lacey's cousin, Trent, got on his knees and pretended to worship her. I laughed. Whoa, talk about cute. Trent has golden brown eyes and kind of long, curly hair that's the same golden brown. He's really tan too. I stared at him—well, marveled is more like it—wondering how he got to be so brown.

"My turn," Richard called, grabbing the stick out of Lacey's hand.

"Bet you can't top that," Lacey said, batting her eyelashes obnoxiously. Then they both laughed, and Richard gave Lacey a playful punch on the shoulder before he took his shot. I don't think I've ever seen Lacey's cheeks glow like that. It was great.

Richard and Lacey have this amazing thing going. They're both infamous for their difficult personalities—Lacey is kind of mean to most people, and Richard is sort of a conceited jerk, especially to girls—so you'd think that putting them together would be a total nightmare. But it isn't. I guess they kind of balance each other out. I remember my mother reading something out loud to me from one of her perfect-relationship-type books. It said something like, "In the best relationships we surprise each other. That's what keeps the relationship exciting. You never know what pleasant surprise is waiting for you just around the corner." Well, even though Richard and Lacey aren't really in a "relationship," at least not yet, they can both be pretty outrageous, so I guess they surprise each other a lot.

Richard was taking forever deciding what shot to take. I glanced over at Trent.

"Come on, man," he said to Richard. "Don't let these girls take us."

"Hey, don't distract me," Richard muttered.

Lacey and I were playing against the boys, and we were winning. I couldn't tell whether it was all an act, and they were really letting us win, or whether we were really playing well.

"So," I said to Trent. "How come you're so tan? Do you go to the beach a lot?"

"Well, no. I live in Berkeley, and there's no beach around there. But I play drums in a reggae band on a boat in San Francisco Bay on the weekends. It gets pretty hot sometimes, so I have to take off my shirt," Trent explained.

I totally blushed. I mean, I seriously couldn't help it.

"So, you're a musician?" I said. "My boyfriend is a musician. Brian. He plays the saxophone. Actually, he's not really my boyfriend anymore."

I bit my lip the minute the words were out of my mouth. *I can't believe I said that. Why did I say that? What is that supposed to mean? He isn't? Since when?* Thankfully, Trent had absolutely no idea what I was talking about.

"Oh?" he said.

"Uh-huh," I replied. I couldn't think of anything normal to say.

"Well, I don't know whether that's good or bad, but I'm glad I get to hang out with you tonight," Trent said. He smiled a warm, golden smile, and I felt glad too.

"You jiggled the table right when I was making my shot," Richard accused Lacey. He had missed his shot completely.

"Did not. You weren't even looking at the balls; that's why you missed," Lacey pointed out.

"I was looking at you," Richard said.

"Oh, you're so sweet," Lacey crooned, batting her eyelashes.

"And I saw you jiggle the table!" Richard said.

"Your turn," Trent told me, stepping aside. I took the pool cue and leaned over the table shakily. If we were winning the game, Lacey was doing it on her own. I was certainly not a very good pool player.

"You might want to loosen up your hold on the cue. Let it slide between your fingers. And bring your elbow back a little more," Trent instructed. He put his hand on my wrist and drew back my arm.

"Now focus your eyes on where you want the ball to go, not on the ball itself."

I did as he instructed, focusing on keeping my

arm relaxed, my eye on the left-corner pocket.

"Now go for it," Trent said.

I took a deep breath and fired away. The ball loomed in the mouth of the pocket for a second, and then it fell.

"Yes!" I shouted. It was the first time I'd ever sunk a ball.

Trent reached out and slapped me five. Then he gave me a little congratulatory pat on the back. "Excellent," he said, his golden brown curls bobbing.

"Now we're in serious trouble." Richard groaned. "Whose idea was this anyway?"

Lacey just winked at me.

I don't know exactly what her wink was for, but I have to admit I was having a great time. I had almost completely forgotten about that thing I'd been so worried about before. What was it again? Oh, that's right—Brian.

I hoped he was having as good a time without me as I was having without him.

Yeah, sure I did.

Brian

"What would you like?" Ken, the barber at Great Waves, asked me. Actually he wasn't really a barber. Barbers are old men in weird lab coats with scissors and combs in their pockets. This guy was only about twenty, and he was dressed like a mechanic. He looked pretty hip. That's why I chose the place. It was supposed to be cutting edge. Ha! Get it? *Cutting edge?*

"Um, I don't know," I said. "I guess just cut it so it looks, um, you know . . . cool."

"One cool cut coming up," Ken said, laughing. I couldn't tell whether he was making fun of me or not. He pumped the barber's chair with his foot so I was sitting high up off the ground, completely defenseless and unable to run.

"Don't worry," Ken said, reaching for the scissors in his pocket. "I'll fix you up."

He started to trim the hair above my forehead, making quick diving and chopping motions at my head with the scissors. I felt my shoulders tense up and stared at my reflection in the mirror. I looked terrified. Then I closed my eyes. This was what I wanted, right? I mean, people always say change is good.

I let my mind wander to band practice—it had me really pumped. I was glad we hadn't changed the words to the song. Salvador had gotten really into the angry-boy thing, and our sound was just getting better and better. And Jessica and Elizabeth had been really impressed too. I couldn't wait for Kristin to hear us. In fact, I couldn't wait to see Kristin again. I hoped she wasn't mad at me for being so grouchy before.

Ken was using an electric razor on the back of my neck now. It felt hot and kind of burned my skin. I kept my eyes shut. Just wait until Kristin saw the new and improved saxophone wizard, the king of pain, Mr. Cutting Edge—Brian the Rainster Rainey.

"Okay, man, you can open your eyes now," I heard Ken say.

I opened them.

My hair was . . . *short.* I mean, it was practically a crew cut. I looked older, I thought. More . . . *intense.*

"Like it?" Ken asked.

Yes. Definitely.

Timeline of Salvador's Activities After Band Practice

6:30 P.M. Salvador calls Anna, asking if she's heard from Elizabeth. Anna says no. "Don't bugeth me," Anna tells Salvador. "I'm memorizing a Shakespearean monologue for drama."

6:35 P.M. Salvador calls Damon and asks for Jessica. "Oh yes. They're out in the backyard, playing with the girls," Damon's mother tells him.

"Is Elizabeth there too?" Salvador asks.

"No, would you like me to get Jessica?" Mrs. Ross asks.

"No, that's all right," Salvador says, and hangs up.

6:38 P.M. Salvador calls the Wakefields and leaves the following message on the answering machine. "Hey, I'm at home, so call me . . . you know . . . whenever. But it's not an emergency or anything. Oh—this is Salvador. I'm calling for Elizabeth. Okay? Um. Okay. Bye."

6:40 P.M. Salvador goes downstairs to ask the Doña if she needs any help with anything. She is wearing big plastic goggles and using a miniblowtorch to weld together a steel amulet for her jewelry-making class. She stares at Salvador through her goggles. Salvador just shrugs and opens the refrigerator door, studying the refrigerator interior closely. He wonders what kind of snacks they have at Blue's house. Fried seaweed? He wonders if Elizabeth might be getting hungry, in which case she might have gone home.

6:44 P.M. Salvador goes back upstairs to call the Wakefields again.

Kristin

I felt a little tired on Wednesday morning after being out on a school night. Not that it was that late—I got home from the Cue Café around seven-thirty. But usually on weeknights I like to lie on my bed and just do my homework and watch TV and talk on the phone with Lacey or Jessica or Brian.

Brian. I couldn't believe it when I got home last night and checked the machine and asked my mom. Brian never even called once. I wondered how band practice went. I wondered if he wished I'd been there. I wondered if he was planning to speak to me today. Or break up with me.

I stuffed my algebra workbook into my bag and slammed my locker shut. I tried to tell myself I didn't really care either way. I'd had a great time last night with Lacey, Richard, and Trent.

"Hey, Kristin," Jessica said, coming up behind me. "Did you have fun last night?"

"Yeah." I shrugged casually. "Lacey's cousin is really nice."

I'm sure Jessica was glad I'd had fun, but I also knew she didn't want to hear the details since Lacey is her least-favorite person on the whole planet. Jessica and Lacey kind of got off to a bad start when Jessica first came to school here, and the tension just never went away. They're like two wrestlers before a match, endlessly bad mouthing each other. It would almost be funny if I wasn't stuck in the middle.

"So did the boys totally beat you at pool?" Jessica asked.

"Nah. Lacey and I beat *them*," I said, smiling. I was actually kind of proud of that fact.

"I bet you did," was all Jessica said. I wondered if she was implying that Lacey had cheated. But I let it go. Lacey does have a reputation for not being the most honest person in the universe. She's even been caught shoplifting. Besides, I've given up trying to get Jessica and Lacey to be friends. If it's going to happen, it's not going to be me that makes it happen.

"Anyway, you missed an awesome practice. Big Noise was totally amazing," Jessica said. "I could barely look at Damon—he's just too cute! And you should have seen Salvador. He was rolling around on the floor and moaning. They have this new song that's actually kind of good. I was surprised."

73

"What about Brian?" I asked.

"Oh, he was way cute too," Jessica said. "Except for his outfit. I mean, I know the baggy-clothes thing is in, but give me a break. What was the deal with that anyway?"

"Um," I said. "I'm not sure. I think maybe he ran out of clean clothes or something."

We started walking toward homeroom. I scanned the hall, looking for Brian, but I didn't see him anywhere.

"Well, anyway, those guys are really getting it together. I can't wait to hear them at the Manchester Club this weekend. I mean, how cool is it to go hear your boyfriend play in his band at the Manchester Club? Even Lacey will be jealous."

Huh?

I kept walking so that Jessica wouldn't think anything was wrong. But I could barely make my legs move, and I was clutching the straps of my backpack way too tightly. Big Noise was playing at the Manchester Club this weekend? So that's what they were doing all this practicing for. And everyone knew all about it. Except me.

My stomach felt oddly hollow, and the faces of my homeroom classmates swam in front of my eyes. My vision settled on Brian, seated at his regular desk by the window. He was wearing the baggy pants again, and his hair was cut really short. He looked completely different.

How had this happened?

Of course, I hadn't seen Brian in the hall. Or talked to him on the phone last night. I didn't recognize him anymore.

In fact, I didn't even know who he was.

Note Thrown in First Period
from Brian to Kristin

Dear Kristin,

Hey! I'm sorry I've been in a bad mood for the past few days. I was wondering if you could come to band practice after school today. There's a song we've been working on that I think you'd like.

Miss you,
—Brian

The note lands under the teacher's desk instead of Kristin's, and Brian has to retrieve it when the bell rings.

Elizabeth

"So what'd you do at Blue's house after we all left?" Salvador asked me. We were sitting at our usual table in the cafeteria. Salvador had finished peeling a nectarine, very slowly, keeping the rind all in one piece. Now he was carefully lining up each juicy section on the table in front of me, like a little orange army.

"We played a few games. Then Leaf's friends came over, and we decided to build a fire in the backyard. We ate marshmallows."

"Humph," Salvador said. "That sounds . . . nice." He looked up from his nectarine, his big, black eyes studying me. "Was it?" he asked, raising his eyebrows.

"Yeah. It was fun," I replied.

Salvador kept staring at me. I took a big sip of my apple juice, ignoring him. He was acting weird. But with Salvador you have to just go with it. I mean, I would be worried if he suddenly started acting *normal*.

"So exactly what kind of games did you play,

you and Blue?" he asked, picking up a nectarine section and holding it in the palm of his hand.

"I can't remember what they're called," I said. I really couldn't.

Salvador closed his fist around the nectarine section and squeezed it until juice was running out between his fingers. "You don't remember?" he said, and raised his eyebrows at me once more.

"Not really," I said. "One had something to do with bugs. You had to fill your boat up with bugs and get them to the island."

Salvador picked up another section of nectarine and did the squeezing thing again. "So you played this bug game, and then?"

"I don't know," I said, starting to get annoyed with him giving me the third degree. "Sal, that's really kind of gross. Are you going to eat that or just kill it?"

Salvador looked up at me again, and this time his eyes looked startled. Then he stared down at the row of nectarine slices, two of which had been massacred by his bare hands. I realized he'd had no idea what he'd been doing.

"Salvador, are you all right?" I asked.

He nodded and reached for my apple juice, gulping it down and crushing the empty juice box in his hand. Then he stood up.

"I'll go get you some more juice," he said, and took off for the drink machine.

I stared after him, amazed. Salvador is an unusual guy, and I've gotten pretty used to his little quirks. But he still manages to surprise me. Every day with Salvador is an adventure. I guess that's why I like him so much. I can't wait to see what he's going to do next.

Brian

I'd meant to talk to Kristin before first period, but she got there late. Then I tried to pass her a note, but my aim was bad. So when I saw her in the lunch line just ahead of me, I walked right up to her.

"Hey," I said, touching her arm. She turned around, her cheeks pink.

"Hey," she said. Her voice was sort of neutral, and she didn't smile at me or anything. "You got a haircut."

I ran my hand over my practically bald head self-consciously. "Yeah. It's pretty short," I said, chuckling.

"So, I hear your band is really coming together," Kristin said, her voice still far away and vacant. "I hear you guys have a new song that everyone is really into." She sounded anything but enthusiastic.

All of a sudden I panicked. What if someone had told Kristin the lyrics to "Too Nice"? Was that why she was acting so . . . cold? I

couldn't exactly invite her to practice now—
that would be like rubbing her nose in it. The
only thing I could think to do was change the
subject.

"Well, it's not that great a song, actually," I
said hastily. "It needs a lot of work. So what did
you do last night?"

"Oh, I had a great time," Kristin said. "Lacey
has this older cousin, Trent, visiting her. He's
amazing. We all went to the Cue Café—Lacey,
me, Richard, and Trent. Trent is really cool. He's
from Berkeley. He plays drums in a reggae band.
He's really good at pool too. My break is so much
better now that he helped me. Lacey and I even
beat the boys."

Kristin was sort of breathless. I guess she'd
really had a good time. "Wow," was all I said in
response.

Kristin paused and looked at me hard, like
she was waiting for me to say something more. I
turned away and reached for the nearest thing
on the lunch counter and put it on my tray. My
mind was working like crazy. So Kristin had
found out all about "Too Nice" and now she was
going out with an older boy called Trent who
played the steel drums or something and was a
whiz at pool. I tried to think of something to
say. I couldn't.

Brian

"Well, see you later," Kristin said stiffly. She walked quickly away to the crowded table where Lacey was sitting with Richard and his friends.

I looked down at my tray. There was a little bowl of cottage cheese sitting on it.

How did that *get there?* I wondered.

Kristin

See, I thought as I marched pur-
posefully across the cafeteria, *I can be as distant
as I want to be. I'm not the huggy, smiley, nice girl
that Brian thinks I am all the time. I'm independent,
full of surprises. If he wants some space, fine. Maybe
I need some space too.*

I carried my tray over to Lacey's table and sat
down in the empty seat next to her. Across the
room Jessica and Damon were sitting alone at a
table, leaning against each other and laughing
hysterically. I wondered why Damon obviously
didn't need any space from Jessica.

"Kristin, listen," Lacey commanded as soon as
I sat down. "You have to come to this barbecue
we're having tomorrow night at our house.
Victoria is driving me insane about it. Can you
believe she actually went out and found black-
and-white metal tiki torches? She says she can't
stand the sight of bamboo, and most tiki torches
are made out of bamboo. As if anyone cares
what the tiki torches are made out of. As if we

can see them anyway—I mean, you only light tiki torches when it's dark out, right?"

Lacey always invites me to family functions to act as a buffer in case her stepmother, Victoria, gets out of hand. Victoria has actually mellowed out lately, with the new baby coming and everything. But she still drives Lacey crazy, especially when she's entertaining. You could say that Victoria has a tendency to put on airs. Okay, she can be really fake. And I have to hand it to Lacey—she's *never* fake. If she doesn't like something or someone, *you know.* Victoria thinks Lacey is rude, and I guess she is. But I love her for it.

"So, Spacey, are you coming or what?" Lacey asked, prodding me on the arm. "Trent will be there," she added.

It's not like I had other plans. Brian certainly wasn't going to ask me over. And I wasn't going to ask him over either. I could just stay at home, but then I would miss seeing Trent again. And I did kind of want to see him again.

"Sure," I agreed. "I'll tell my mom about it tonight."

"Good," Lacey said, passing me half of her chocolate cupcake. She licked the frosting on her half. "Trent has been talking about you, you know."

I took the cupcake half and put it on my tray for later. "He has? Like how?" I asked.

"Oh, he wanted to know if you still had a boyfriend," Lacey said, grinning mischievously.

"And?" I asked.

"And I told him not really," Lacey said, not meeting my gaze. She knew she was in trouble.

I was about to start in on her, but then I changed my mind. Instead I just picked up my half of the cupcake and took a huge bite.

"Good," I said, with my mouth full.

Lacey stared at me, wide-eyed. I guess Brian isn't the only one who's full of surprises.

Salvador

"Your great-uncle Hector was a singer, you know," the Doña told me. She was just pulling into Blue's driveway to drop me off for practice. "He had eight wives," she added, winking at me.

"Wow," I said.

"Yes. And he wore a tie every day, for all occasions, even to get the paper. He said he could never be sure when he was going to meet his next wife."

I felt kind of bad for Uncle Hector's wives— always on the verge of being replaced. He sounded like kind of a jerk.

"Was he a good singer?" I asked my grandmother.

"Yes. He was a very good singer. Very popular." The Doña pulled to a stop and reached for her purse in the backseat. She fished around in it and finally pulled out a little container of mints, which she offered to me. "Hector believed a singer should always have fresh breath," she told me.

"Thanks," I said, taking one before I got out of the car. "I'll call you when I'm done."

The other three guys were already there, warming up.

"Hey." I gave Damon a high five.

Blue was pitter-pattering on his drums. I flashed him a is-something-going-on-between-you-and-Elizabeth? suspicious look, but he just beamed right back at me, the same happy-go-lucky, open-faced Blue as ever. If he was hiding something, he was unbelievably good at it.

Brian looked like he was holding his breath. His face was all red, and he was staring at the floor without blinking.

I smiled at him and said, "Hey," but Brian just glared back.

Cool, I thought, *maybe we'll come up with another awesome song.* After all, "Too Nice" came out of one of Brian's dark moods.

"What's up, Brian?" I asked. "Trouble with Kristin again?"

Brian kept glaring.

"Are you guys fighting?" I pressed.

Brian blinked and took a deep breath. "Yeah, I guess."

I picked up the microphone. "We started to fight . . . ," I snarled into it.

Brian's glare returned.

"Salvador," Damon warned. "Easy."

"I'm just asking," I said. "'Cause I like to sing about heartache. That's right, baby," I sang into the mike, imitating Elvis.

"Salvador!" Damon commanded. "Hey, Brian. It's all right. You can tell us the deal. What happened?"

Brian looked unsure. "Um," he said. "I think Kristin may be interested in some other guy. She told me all about what a great time she had with him last night. It kind of . . . threw me, I guess."

Damon, Blue, and I exchanged glances, maintaining a respectful silence.

Then I broke the ice.

"Oldest trick in the book," I said. "She just wants to make you jealous. Mentioning another guy is like the number-one classic make-him-jealous scenario."

Brian looked at his shoes. I was kind of proud of myself for being so good at giving manly advice. Although I wasn't sure if I knew what I was talking about. I mean, I've only had a girlfriend once, for just a week. And it was only Anna. It was back when I still had a crush on Elizabeth, but Anna had been really upset about something, and somehow we just wound up kissing. It was a sympathy kiss, not a kiss kiss, but we went out for a week anyway. . . . No, I really shouldn't be giving out relationship advice. I had absolutely no worthwhile experience whatsoever. I mean, who did I think I was, my great-uncle Hector?

"But why would Kristin want me to be jealous?" Brian asked, sounding completely baffled.

"Because now that you're playing with Big Noise, you're like this cool rock-star guy. Kristin's just scared you're going to run off with one of our groupies or something," Blue said excitedly. He did a little *ka-ching-boom-ching* thing on his cymbals.

I could tell by the look on Brian's face that we probably weren't going to get a song out of this one.

Brian

I'd never heard anything more stupid in my entire life.

"Wait a minute. Let's get one thing straight," I said angrily, looking around the garage at my wide-eyed band mates. "I am not a rock star. And neither is anyone else in this room. Not even close. We have one halfway decent song, and that's it."

The other three guys looked down at their feet like I had completely burst their bubble. I'm sorry, but it needed bursting. *Groupies?* Yeah, right.

I waited for one of them to say something, but they just kept quiet, not meeting my gaze. I ran my hand over my close-cropped hair and shifted from foot to foot. Then I went over and picked up my sax.

"Okay, come on. Let's start practicing. We still have a gig on Saturday," I said lamely.

Salvador glanced at Blue and cleared his throat. Blue sat up straight behind his drum set and cracked his knuckles. Damon hitched his guitar strap around his neck and put the fingers of his left hand on the frets.

"All right," Salvador said. Actually he was whispering. The mike was the only reason I could hear him. "Let's run through 'Too Nice.'"

Blue tapped his sticks together, getting us all on the beat, and then we began to play.

"You say I'm too nice, but I disagree . . . ," Salvador sang in that same lifeless whisper.

I honked my sax, Damon twanged his guitar, and Blue bonked his drums and cymbals. It was as if we were playing in zero gravity, like astronauts in a spaceship. Our instruments were floating in the air in front of us, and everything was very slow and difficult. We sounded terrible.

"I'm taking back my CDs, eatin' pizza, extra cheese . . ."

"Too Nice" is the kind of song you can only play with a sort of ironic anger that's hard to pull off when you're genuinely in a bad mood. It wasn't working for us right now; that much was definitely clear.

Suddenly Damon stopped playing. Then Blue followed suit. I let up on my sax, and only Salvador was left whispering into the mike.

"You say I'm too nice—" Salvador broke off

and stuck his hands in his pockets. "What's up, guys?" he asked.

"Why don't we sleep this off and give it another try tomorrow?" Damon suggested. "I don't think we've got it today."

"Sounds good to me," Blue said. "I told Leaf I'd cook us black-bean quiche for dinner tonight anyway. It takes a while."

"I'm going to have to call my grandmother to tell her to come get me," Salvador said. "Can I use your phone?"

"Sure," Blue said. "I'll show you where it is."

I just shrugged and put my sax back in its case. It was obvious that I'd ruined practice with what I'd said. But if these guys couldn't take a little reality check, that was their problem.

"All right," I said, heading for the door. "See you."

"Hey, want a ride home, Brian?" Salvador called from behind me.

"Nah," I said, turning around. "Thanks. I think I'll walk." Then I turned back around and left.

I walked down Blue's driveway, kicking at stones and little sticks in my path. The low-lying evening sun felt hot on my head, and I ran my hand over my hair. This rubbing-my-head thing was getting to be a new habit of mine. As I walked, I thought about how amazing it is that you can change so much in so little time—your clothes, your hair, your habits, your hobbies, your friends . . . your girlfriends. Or in Kristin's case, your *boyfriends.*

I turned down Beach Road, heading toward home. My mind was still working. I tried to remember how and when this thing with Kristin had started. We'd hardly spoken in the last few days, but we'd never had a fight or anything. Okay, so I'd been a little testy recently, but Kristin could have been a bit more sensitive too. When I *really* thought about it, it was the *song* that had started all the trouble. If I hadn't been worried that Kristin would be upset if she heard the lyrics to "Too Nice," then I would have invited her to practice, and she would never have spent the whole night playing pool with some older guy from a Berkeley reggae band. And how long was I planning to keep the song a secret from Kristin anyway? "Too Nice" had caused way too much trouble already. And it was *too* not worth it.

I cut across the playing fields behind the high school, taking the shortcut back to my house. As soon as I got home, I started rewriting the lyrics to the song. The other guys would just have to live with that. If the lyrics to "Too Nice" were actually *nicer,* then I wouldn't have to worry about Kristin hearing them and then things could get back to normal with us again.

Change may be good, but not going out with or even being friends with Kristin—that wasn't the kind of change I wanted to make.

Salvador

"So," I said to Blue while we waited on his stoop for the Doña to come pick me up. There was sort of an unspoken assumption that we were absolutely not going to talk about the horrible practice we'd just had. "Elizabeth said she really liked the song."

I studied Blue's profile to see how he reacted when I said Elizabeth's name. Blue tilted his face up to the sun and closed his eyes, basking.

"Yeah. She told me," he said. "She said it was cool we were trying something different."

Okay, that didn't tell me much. But I couldn't just come right out and ask, "So, do you *like* Elizabeth?" Could I?

"Yeah. Elizabeth is the coolest, you know?" Blue went on. "It's like she never has anything negative to say. She's just all good, and beautiful too. I love that."

I stared at him some more. Luckily he still had his eyes closed. I wondered if he was daydreaming about Elizabeth as we spoke.

I guess I had my answer. Blue definitely liked Elizabeth. A lot.

I peered down the driveway. *Where is my grandmother anyway?* I wondered. She was usually such a major speed demon, but she sure was taking her time getting here. I didn't want to hang out with Blue anymore. I really didn't need to hear him tell me how wonderful Elizabeth was. I already knew.

What I didn't know was why just hearing Blue say Elizabeth's name bothered me so much. Elizabeth is my friend, so of course I like her a lot. But I don't *like* her. I got over that a long time ago, didn't I?

Maybe not.

It was the first time in a very long time that I'd even allowed myself to think that maybe I really did *like* Elizabeth. But I knew that she absolutely didn't *like* me.

"Well, I think I'll let you get started on that dinner. I'm going to walk down and meet my grandmother at the end of the driveway," I told Blue. I stood up and dusted off the seat of my jeans.

Blue opened his eyes and blinked. "Okay. See you at school tomorrow," he said.

"See you," I said, and started walking toward the orange-and-white mailbox at the end of Blue and Leaf's driveway. My grandmother's car blasted around the corner just then and braked with a squeal. I walked out to meet her.

I got into the passenger seat and slammed the door shut.

"Good practice?" the Doña asked.

I shrugged and looked out my window.

"Oh, I remembered something else your great-uncle Hector always used to say that I thought I should tell you," the Doña said, pulling a U-ey. "He said you must always act on your feelings. If you keep the emotions all locked up inside, your singing voice won't be pure."

I kept looking out my window. "Just drive," I said.

"Think Twice"
("Too Nice" revised)

I saved you a place
And the cheesiest slice,
Got you a diet soda
In the brand that you like.
Who else knows you this well?
Who'd think of such things?
Please think twice
before you turn your back on me.

Chorus:
We're best friends,
We meet after school;
We talk on the phone,
We say what we feel.

Second Chorus:
So don't forget to think
Before you say you're better off
Without me,
Because I know I'm twice as good
When I'm together with you,
Think twice.
Think twice.

Thursday, SVJH Class Notes

Salvador to Elizabeth

Hey, Liz.
   I saw you looking out the window. It's really pretty out, isn't it? I wish we could go outside and roll around in the grass like dogs. Don't you?

Love,
Salvador

Elizabeth to Salvador

You are crazy.

Elizabeth to Anna

Dear Anna,
   I think Salvador is acting kind of funny. I mean, really strange. Not just Salvador strange. Have you noticed it too? Is there something going on with him that I don't know about? Not that you have to tell me. I'm just worried. He's making me nervous.

Anna to Elizabeth

The Doña probably changed his diet.
Maybe he's getting too much protein or
something. Give him a few days to adjust.
And don't worry, I'm not withholding any
juicy information. Your guess is as good
as mine. But don't forget, Salvador is,
and always will be, a freak.

Blue to Elizabeth

Hey, Liz,
   If you're into it, you could drop by after band
practice today and we could take the boards out.
It's a beautiful day, so I bet the sunset is going
to be rad, rad, rad. I'm going surfing anyway, so
come with me if you want.
                    See ya!
                    Blue

Elizabeth to Blue

Thanks. I'd love to.

Kristin

I got to Lacey's house just as the balsamic pickled-onion glazed Japanese beef was being thrown on the hickory-laced barbecue.

"Oh, hello, Kristin," Victoria said, opening the door for me. "Would you like to try some scampi?" She held out a platter of very big shrimp with googly eyes and antennae. They were all lined up neatly on a bed of sliced avocados and endive, like something out of a gourmet magazine. It looked like Victoria had been taking her cooking classes pretty seriously. I didn't want to hurt her feelings, so I took one.

"Thanks," I said. I put it on the little white paper cocktail napkin with *Frells* stamped on it in blue and held it in the palm of my hand. Those bug eyes were so weird. I wouldn't have been surprised if the shrimp stood up and did a little song and dance, like the Cricket in Times Square.

"Lacey's out back, entertaining Richard," Victoria said. "Why don't you go join her?" She smiled at me. Victoria's smile always wound up looking like a smirk, but at least she tried.

"Okay," I said. I hesitated. "That dress looks nice on you," I added. I don't even know why I said it, but Victoria is pregnant and has a big belly now. I'm sure she's feeling kind of self-conscious. And she actually did look pretty. Usually she's all straight edges and neat lines, but when a woman is pregnant, she always looks a little softer. It was really being pregnant that suited Victoria, not her dress.

She touched her stomach and actually smiled a genuine, smirkless smile.

"Why, thank you, Kristin," she said. Then, before she could get too emotional, she stuffed a scampi in her mouth and headed into the kitchen.

A few of the Frellses' friends were standing around the food table in the backyard, but there was no one I knew. Then I spotted Lacey and Richard, over by the stone wall bordering the yard.

"Hey, Kristin," Lacey said when she saw me. She was wearing a denim halter dress that revealed most of her bare back and had her hair pulled up in a messy pile on top of her head. Obviously Victoria had no say in how Lacey presented herself. Richard was standing beside her, grinning.

"What's up?" Richard said. He tilted back his soda glass and took in a mouthful of ice, crushing it noisily with his teeth. Then he dropped an ice cube on Lacey's shoulder blade, and she leaped forward, shrieking.

I felt kind of uncomfortable. Lacey seemed perfectly happy hanging out with Richard—I didn't know why she'd wanted me to come. There was no one else to talk to either except the scampi, which I was still holding.

"Trent is around here somewhere," Lacey said. "He'll be so glad you came."

"Yeah," I said, shrugging as if to imply that I really didn't care. I was only there because Lacey had asked me to come, not because I thought Trent and I had any . . . *whatever.*

As a matter of fact, I'd spent the whole day at school keeping pretty much to myself, thinking. Not about Trent, but about Brian. My best friend, my boyfriend, my *Brian.* I couldn't believe we were barely speaking now. It didn't make any sense. All I wanted was to apologize to him, and make up, and forget about it. But the more I thought about it, I couldn't remember what had started this whole mess in the first place. Then I realized that it wasn't that I couldn't remember; it was that I didn't know. I had no idea. And how can you apologize for something when you have no idea what you're apologizing for?

"Are you going to eat that?" Richard asked. He pointed at the scampi in my hand. I shook my head and held it out to him. He took it and popped it in his mouth.

"Gross," Lacey said in disgust. "Uh-oh," she added, raising her eyebrows and looking off over my shoulder. She grabbed my arm and pinched it, and I turned to see what she was looking at.

It was Trent, standing by the smoking grill, holding hands with Tamara Sonnenheim, Lacey's sixteen-year-old neighbor. He held up his hand and waved to us and then turned to listen to something Tamara was saying.

"Guess Trent couldn't wait for you to break up with Brian," Lacey said, shrugging. I could feel her watching me to see how I'd react.

The funny thing is, I didn't feel anything. And why should I? I'd met Trent once and we'd had a fun time, but I had no expectations. Besides, he lived in another town. And besides that, I *hadn't* broken up with Brian, and I didn't intend to either. If he wanted out of this relationship, he would have to be the one to break up with me.

"Lacey," I said seriously. "Don't even talk

about me and Brian breaking up like that. I'm not breaking up with him."

"Then what are you doing?" Lacey asked.

"I don't know," I said miserably. *Thanks for rubbing it in,* I thought. My eyes started to lose focus, and my chin was trembling. Richard had wandered off to find more scampi, thank God. The last thing I wanted to do was burst into tears in front of everyone in the Frellses' backyard.

Lacey looked at her watch. "Listen, Kristin. This is ridiculous," she said impatiently.

"Sorry," I said, and wiped my nose on my sleeve.

"Look, it's early," Lacey said. "I bet the guys are still practicing over in Blue's garage. And I'm sure you don't *really* want to hang out with my uptight, pregnant stepmother and her phony friends. Why don't you go try and talk to Brian? You and he are like the only people in the world born without the gene for meanness—how long can this go on? If you ask me, it's getting really boring."

"But—," I started to say.

"Please," Lacey interrupted. "How am I going to eat my grilled salmon shish kebabs with you here, acting all pathetic?"

"Really?" I sniffed.

"Yes, really," Lacey said with pretend annoyance. "Please spare me the misery and *go*. We can call you a cab."

Leave it to Lacey to give me hope. I threw my arms around her. "Thanks, Lacey," I said, really crying now. "You're the best."

Lacey sighed. "I know," she said.

Brian

"Hey, Brian," Damon said when I walked into Blue's garage on Thursday afternoon, clutching the lyrics for "Think Twice" in my hand. He looked really glad to see me. I guess after yesterday they thought I might quit or something. "Blue's upstairs getting sodas. He'll be right down."

"Brian!" Salvador shouted. He was hanging upside down, his long legs dangling over Leaf's pull-up bar. "You should try this. It's very stimulating. I think all artists should hang upside down before they start to work." He paused. "Not that we're artists or anything."

I cleared my throat. They were both being supernice to me. *Just wait until I tell them I'm changing our best song,* I thought.

I really didn't know how I was going to do it. The guys were so into "Too Nice." How was I going to tell them I'd rewritten it completely? It even had a different title. What if they hated it? What if they made fun of me? What if they just flat out refused to play it?

I didn't care. I hadn't stayed up late rewriting the song for *them,* had I?

Blue clip-clapped down the stairs in his flip-flops. "Hey, Brian," he said. "Orange or root beer?"

"Uh, orange," I said.

Blue tossed me a can and handed Damon his. "Salvador, I don't think you can drink yours like that," he said. "What are you, a bat?"

Damon pointed at the piece of paper in my hand. "What's that?" he asked. "A new song?"

I took a gulp of my soda. "Kind of," I said lamely. "Actually, I sort of changed the lyrics to, um, 'Too Nice,' you know, because I thought they were, um, kind of too mean?"

Salvador crashed to the floor and then stood up, scratching his curly black head.

All three guys stared at me.

"Whoa," Blue said. "Dude, the gig is the day after tomorrow."

"I know," I said.

"We have enough to worry about," Damon said. "Why do you want to mess up a good thing?"

"I don't know," I said.

"You what?" Salvador said. "But that song rocks. What'd you change it for?"

I stared at the floor, trying to come up with an answer that would satisfy them. I couldn't think of anything.

"I didn't want Kristin to hear those other lyrics," I admitted. "Okay?"

"Dude," Blue said. "Why not?"

"Because," I explained, "I don't think she'd like it. I think she'd be upset."

"Okay," Damon said. "But it's just a song. It's fiction."

"Totally," Salvador said. "It was inspired by real events, but so is all good stuff. You can't dwell on that. You can't kill the song because of that. It's not fair to the song."

As usual, Salvador was being melodramatic.

"Look, can we just try it?" I asked, handing him the lyrics.

"'Think Twice,'" Salvador read. "What's that supposed to mean?"

"Uh, it's about thinking twice before you dis your friends, or your girlfriends, or whatever," I explained.

"Yeah, whatever," Salvador grumbled. "Who do you think we are—'N Sync?"

"It doesn't rhyme, does it?" Damon asked.

"The tune's still the same, right?" Blue chimed in.

"Hey. Let's just try it once. If it doesn't work, we'll drop it, okay?" I pleaded. I picked up my

109

sax, adjusted the strap, and waited for them to get ready.

"Fine," Salvador said. He carried the piece of paper with the lyrics written on it over to the microphone. "Let's just do this."

Blue walked over to his drum set and sat down. Damon slung his guitar strap over his shoulder. I'd never seen them look so glum.

"I saved you a place and the cheesiest slice . . . ," Salvador sang, his voice doleful and low. He sounded like his dog just died. "Got you a diet soda in the brand that you like . . ."

I played along, nice and easy. Damon did a little riff on the guitar—nothing too hard, just an elaboration on the melody. Blue kept the beat going. It was fine. Mellow. Nothing earth-shattering, but fine.

Salvador did a little body wave with a spin, obviously imitating the choreographed moves all those cheesy boy bands use. Then he grabbed the mike and started to snarl, "Let me give you some advice—don't you mess with me!" breaking into "Too Nice" with all his pent-up energy.

The other guys started going nuts too, and I followed suit. I couldn't help it. It was irresistible.

Kristin

I could hear the guys playing when the cab pulled into Blue's driveway. It was really loud—no wonder they're called Big Noise. Good thing Blue's neighbors don't live too close.

I paid the driver and got out of the cab. I figured Brian and the others probably couldn't hear me since they didn't stop playing or anything. I walked around the side of the garage to the entrance to where, in a normal household, the cars are supposed to be kept. But Leaf keeps his car outside so that part of the garage is the surf shop. There were eight surfboards leaning against the wall, and a wooden table set up in the middle of the room with melted wax stuck all over it, and a vise to hold the boards. A donkey piñata hung from the ceiling. I pulled a foil-wrapped piece of chocolate out of the hole in its side and turned it over in my hands. I wondered if Blue and Leaf ever ate regular food or just chocolate and ice cream and potato chips and soda for every meal, every day. If I didn't have a mother who fed me soy burgers and broccoli and herbal tea all the time, that's what I'd eat.

As I stood there, shuffling my feet and thinking, I realized I was dawdling. I guess I was kind of nervous about just showing up there. I mean, it was going to be pretty obvious that I was there to see Brian. And it sounded like they were really into their rehearsal. I didn't want to interrupt their flow. So I decided to hang back and wait until they were done. They were playing in the next room—the workroom. But I could hear them loud and clear from where I was.

"All this nice may be nice for you, but it's not nice for me . . . ," I heard Salvador sing angrily.

Nice, I mused. *That's funny. I'm always telling Brian he's too nice.*

"I'm taking back my CDs, eatin' pizza, extra cheese, I'm playing games with the boys. . . ."

Wait a minute, I thought.

Brian never gets extra cheese if we're sharing a pizza, but if he just has his own slice, he always gets it. And I've borrowed a million

CDs from him, and I always forget to return them.

My ears started to feel like they were on fire, and I could feel my face turning bright red.

Was this song about us?

"Say good-bye to Mr. Nice, yeah, he's hittin' the road; find some other guy to step on 'cause I'm in a new mode!"

Yep, I was sure of it. I tried to keep my hands from trembling as I backed away from the workroom door. I had to get out of here. Because if I was right, it sounded like there was no more *us*. So Brian really had been planning to break up with me! But why hadn't he just come right out with it and told me instead of writing a song about it? Was he waiting for me to find out when I heard the song at the Manchester Club? How twisted could you get? It was like one of those romantic proposals you hear about—like having "Marry me?" put up on the scoreboard at a football game—except in reverse.

I tossed the piece of chocolate on the ground and headed back out to the driveway. The last thing I wanted was for Brian to find me there, listening in on his freedom-from-me song. I started to run and bumped into one of Blue's surfboards, sending it crashing to the floor. I sprinted down the driveway and back toward home, angry tears streaming down my face.

I couldn't believe Brian had written a song about how much he hated me. I hoped he was satisfied. He could choke on that extra cheese for all I cared.

Brian

When we heard the crash, we all stopped playing. Blue stood up and ran out to see if one of his surfboards had gotten hurt.

"Whoa!" we heard him yell. "Hey, wait up!"

The rest of us dropped our instruments and followed him. Blue was out in the driveway.

"What the—?" Salvador said.

"What's going on?" Damon asked as we walked out to join Blue.

Was it a burglar? I wondered, my heart pounding.

But when we reached him, Blue turned to me, wearing the world's biggest frown. "It was Kristin."

All of a sudden I had a perfect picture in my mind of what had just happened. Kristin had come over, heard us singing that stupid, stupid song, and got so upset, she ran away.

There was an awkward silence.

"That's it," I said. "If we don't play the song the way I rewrote it, then I quit. You can find

115

another sax player if you want to, but I am not getting up onstage Saturday and playing 'Too Nice.' It's just not worth it. It's got to be 'Think Twice' or nothing."

I took a deep breath and stared down my band mates.

"Deal," Damon said. He held out his hand, and I shook it. Limply.

"Deal," Blue said, slapping me five. Weakly.

"Oh, okay. Yeah. I guess. Why not?" Salvador said. He made an *X* in the dirt with his toe, traced a circle around it, and stamped on it. "Deal."

Great—they all agreed. Now I just needed to explain everything to Kristin. If she'd even talk to me.

Elizabeth

"Watch out for the undertow," my big brother, Steven, said when he dropped me off at Blue's house.

"Thanks," I said. "I'll do that." I got out of the car, threw my beach towel over my arm, and closed the door.

"And sharks!" Steven yelled out his window as he pulled away.

That's what I love about my brother. He amuses himself so easily.

I could hear the boys still playing in the garage. *Cool,* I thought. I loved their new song. And Salvador looked so funny last time, growling those angry lyrics while he rolled around on the floor like Mick Jagger or somebody. I strolled through the back area where Blue and Leaf keep their surfboards and leaned against the doorway to the workroom.

"We're best friends, we meet after school . . . ," Salvador was singing. It sounded like the same tune as the song I liked, but the lyrics were

117

different from what I remembered. And Salvador wasn't writhing around on the floor. He was standing with one hand in his pocket, holding a piece of paper in the other, reading the lyrics from it.

"We talk on the phone, we say what we feel. . . ." Salvador made a face as he sang, like he was eating something that tasted truly awful.

I stayed where I was and listened to them finish up the song. It wasn't just Salvador who wasn't into it. The other boys were playing like they were half asleep, even Blue. I'd never heard anything more lifeless. They were murdering the song. But the song itself wasn't so bad. The lyrics were sweet, adorable. What was wrong with them?

Salvador squeezed out the last lines of the chorus and spun around, dropping the mike on the floor. His face lit up when he saw me. And then he frowned.

"Hello, Elizabeth," he said. "What're *you* doing here?" His voice sounded accusing, like he wasn't happy to see me after all.

"Hey, Liz," Blue called out, beaming his Blue-est smile at me. "Glad you could make it."

Brian and Damon started putting away their instruments. I clutched my towel to my chest. "You don't have to stop playing because I'm here," I said, suddenly uncomfortable. I could feel Salvador's big, black eyes staring me down.

"Why *are* you here?" Salvador asked. I stared at him. Did he know how rude that sounded? I hoped so.

"Um . . . ," I started to say.

"We're going surfing," Blue explained. "Don't worry, Elizabeth, I think we were ready to call it a day anyway, right, guys?"

Brian barely looked at me. He mumbled something, but I couldn't hear what he said. Then he stalked out of the garage with his saxophone still strapped around his neck. Was he going to walk home like that? With that short haircut, those enormous pants, and his saxophone, Brian looked a little crazy. I don't know; maybe that was the look he was going for.

"Hey, Liz, I'll see you later. Jessica's coming over to help me baby-sit," Damon said. He snapped his guitar case shut and walked out without even a "see ya" to the other guys.

It wasn't exactly the kind of unity four friends playing in a band for fun would be expected to display.

That left me with Salvador and Blue. Who were both staring at me with scary smiles plastered to their faces.

Blue clapped. "Right on!" he yelled at me,

way too enthusiastically. "Let's go surfing!"

Salvador looked at his watch. "The Doña's probably waiting for me," he mumbled. "Call me, okay, Elizabeth?" he said, like we had something really important to discuss.

I shrugged. "Okay."

Then Salvador walked out of the garage without even looking at Blue.

"What's going on?" I asked Blue. "Did you guys have a fight or something?"

Blue cracked his knuckles and pulled off his T-shirt so all he was wearing was his orange-and-blue board shorts. "Nah," he said without smiling. "Come on, the water's waiting."

He ducked into the next room to get our boards.

I guessed Big Noise was having big problems.

Messages on Kristin Seltzer's Answering Machine

Beep.

"*Hola*, Kristin, this is Trent. You know, Lacey's cousin? Hey, I was wondering if maybe you wanted to hang out on Saturday night? I'm leaving on Sunday, and I'd like to see you again before I go. Give me a call, okay? It's Lacey's number, so you know it, right? See you later."

—Played back once.

Beep.

"Kristin. Hi, it's me. Brian. Rainey. Um. I guess you probably know that our band is playing Saturday night. At the Manchester Club. Um. I'd really like it if you came. Um. You probably don't want to. It's not a big deal. I just thought I'd see if you could make it. Anyway, I'll see you at school tomorrow, okay? Bye."

—Played back four times.

Kristin

"Oh, hello, Kristin," Mr. Frells said stiffly. "I'm sure Lacey's very eager to talk to you. Why don't you call her on her line?"

"Oh, actually I didn't want to speak to Lacey. I'm calling for Trent. Is he there?" I asked. I wound the phone cord around my waist and opened the freezer door just for something to do.

"Aha," Mr. Frells said. "Yes. Yes, he is. Just a minute." He put me on hold. I stared at the stack of ice-cube trays and the lonely mint-chocolate-chip ice-cream carton in our freezer. I hate mint chocolate chip. I closed the freezer door and opened the refrigerator.

"Kristin!" I heard my mother call from her bedroom. "I'm just finishing this letter. I'll get dinner in a minute."

"Okay, Mom!" I yelled back. If my mom knew I was even thinking of going out with an older guy, with a car, no less, she'd probably flip. I wasn't going to *lie*, exactly. I just didn't plan on mentioning it.

"Kristin?" Trent's voice said into the phone.

"Hi," I said, my face suddenly burning up.

"So, do you want to do something Saturday?" he asked.

"Sure," I said.

"Okay, so I'll pick you up at, like, six? I thought we could play minigolf. I saw this place down by the beach."

"Okay," I said again. "I'll see you then."

"Bye," we both said, and hung up.

I blew out a huge breath. It wasn't exactly relief I was feeling; I was just glad I'd stuck to my guns. I knew that Trent was obviously a player—I mean, what happened to Tamara Sonnenheim, right? I wasn't interested in Trent.

I opened the freezer again and took out the mint-chocolate-chip ice cream. I grabbed a spoon, pulled the lid off the carton, wedged off a frozen spoonful, and put it in my mouth. It was actually kind of good. I liked the way the ice cream melted instantly when it hit my tongue and the bittersweet chocolate chips were left to chew on afterward. I took another spoonful.

One thing was for sure. I was not going to give Brian any satisfaction by showing up at the Manchester Club to hear him play his breakup song to me.

Kristin

I heard my mother coming out of her bedroom and put the ice cream back into the freezer, slamming the door shut just in time.

If Brian wanted to break up with me, he'd have to tell me to my face.

Elizabeth

"Hi, it's me. You wanted me to call?" I said to Salvador that night when I got back from surfing. I took a big bite of my macaroni and cheese. My mom had let me take my dinner upstairs to my room since Jessica was out with Damon and Steven was at his SAT class. My parents try to get us all to eat together most nights, but sometimes it just doesn't work out.

"Hello," Salvador said. "How was surfing?"

"Fine," I said. "The sunset was really pretty, but it got dark after like half an hour, and Blue said he had a quiz to study for, so I just called my mom to pick me up. Anyway, what did you want me to call you about?" I asked, chewing loudly. Normally I'm not that gross when I talk to people on the phone, but with Salvador it doesn't really matter. I knew he wouldn't think I was being revolting.

"I . . . ," Salvador said. "Well, I didn't really have a particular thing to tell you. I just, you know, thought we could, like, talk. You know, like we normally do," he said.

"Right," I said. As if the conversation we were having was normal. "Well, could you put your grandmother on for a second?" I asked. "I wanted to get her recipe for oatmeal cookies."

"Yes, of course," Salvador said. He sounded almost relieved not to have to talk to me. "Great. I'll put her on. Doña? Elizabeth wants to talk to you. Okay, here she is. See you tomorrow, Elizabeth."

"Elizabeth?" the Doña said. "Are you studying hard?"

"Well, not too hard." I laughed. Everyone is always worried that I work too hard at school. But I have plenty of time for fun. I mean, I'm only in eighth grade; it's not like I have a ton of homework yet.

"Salvador never seems to do any homework," she said. "All he does is bother me. He's a real nuisance."

"Yes," I agreed. "He is. Um, I was wondering if you could give me your recipe for oatmeal cookies. I love your oatmeal cookies."

"Just follow the recipe on the back of the oats container," she instructed. "Then add a teaspoon of allspice to the dough and a cup of coconut. That's my special secret."

"I won't tell anyone," I promised.

"You're a good girl," the Doña said. "It's no wonder Salvador likes you so much. You two are so different, but together you are like puzzle pieces that fit together just right. I—"

There was a shuffling and a grappling sound. The Doña dropped the phone.

"Hello?" I said. "Is everything all right?"

Salvador

"Hello?" Elizabeth's worried voice rang out from the phone receiver, which was sitting in a colander full of potato peelings in the kitchen sink, where it had landed when I made a grab for it.

The Doña was glaring at me, bulldoglike.

"Go away," I whispered at her, and dove for the phone. "Elizabeth?"

"Salvador?" she said. "What happened to your grandmother? Is she all right?"

"Oh yes, she's fine," I said, flapping my hands at my grandmother, who was still standing there with her hands on her hips. "A pot boiled over on the stove, and she had to make a run for it. Sorry about that."

"Well, okay, but I think she was in the middle of telling me something. Is she coming back?"

"No," I said decisively. "She had to go out to the garage to get the onions. We keep our onions and our potatoes in the garage, where it's cool." My grandmother's eyes narrowed, and she shook her head. The Doña hates liars.

"Okay," Elizabeth said. "Well, when she comes back, can you put her back on? I want to ask her what allspice is."

"All what?" I asked.

"Allspice."

"Oh," I said, and hesitated. That didn't sound too bad. But there was no way I was going to put my grandmother back on the phone. "Okay," I told Elizabeth. "Actually, I'd better go help her. But I'll have her call you." I was too humiliated to continue this ridiculous conversation.

After I hung up the phone, I flashed my grandmother the meanest look I could muster and left the room before she could yell at me for my rude behavior. As it was, I had enough to worry about. *Puzzle pieces?* Please.

Friday

8:30 A.M. Kristin and Lacey are talking at Kristin's locker. Brian walks purposefully toward them, and they head into the ladies' room.

9:07 A.M. Salvador tries to get Elizabeth's attention in English, but Mrs. Bertram, Elizabeth, and Anna launch into an in-depth discussion about Jane's decision to marry Mr. Rochester in *Jane Eyre*. Salvador raises his hand and says he can't believe the old guy still gets Jane, even when he's burnt to a crisp and crippled. Elizabeth glares at him.

12:00 P.M. Blue and Damon unwrap their sandwiches in glum silence on the school steps. Jessica joins them and does all the talking.

12:15 P.M. Elizabeth sits down with Anna and Salvador at their usual table at lunch. She pulls her lunch out of her bag and offers her friends the oatmeal cookies she baked last night. Salvador takes a cookie, his cheeks turning red. Elizabeth and Anna start in on

Jane Eyre again, taking no notice of Salvador.

12:17 P.M. At lunch Brian heads for the table where Ronald Rheece is sitting with the debate team. He needs some time to think, which means he needs some time away from his friends. Unfortunately, Ronald's table is in the middle of a heated debate about fashion. Ronald's side has taken the argument that clothes are a tool for self-expression. Marlee Randall's side claims that kids who follow the latest trends are just victims of advertising. Brian sweeps his hand over his new haircut, hitches up his baggy pants, sits down, and tries to pretend he's somewhere else.

12:17 P.M. Kristin sees Brian walk past her on the lunch line and pretends not to notice him. *But did he see me?* she wonders. She keeps letting people cut in front of her, hoping Lacey will show up soon so she has someone to eat lunch with. The eighth-grade vice president, Bethel McCoy, taps her on the shoulder and offers to share her leftover veggie lasagna with Kristin. Kristin practically hugs her.

2:30 P.M. The final bell rings and everyone goes home, with no plans to see each other later.

Kristin

I tugged at the hem of the black wraparound V-necked sweater Lacey had persuaded me to buy at the mall that afternoon and checked myself out in the full-length mirror. I looked good, I guess. I walked over to my bed and flopped down on my back. It was Saturday night. Brian and the other boys in Big Noise were getting ready to play their gig at the Manchester Club. A lot of other bands were going to be playing tonight too. Everyone else my age in the whole school was going, probably in the whole town. While I was getting ready to go out with an older boy I didn't really even know or like all that much. When I thought about it, I didn't really want to go out at all. I wanted to put on my pink-heart pajamas and crawl under the covers and read all my old children's books.

I got up and walked over to the mirror again and studied myself. I had left my hair down, put on smoky pink lip gloss, and dressed in all black. Lacey would be proud.

I fussed with the black sweater. It felt a little tight and looked a little too . . . black.

What was I doing? Nothing I wanted to be doing—that much I knew. I was supposed to be at the Manchester Club.

Without stopping to think, I grabbed the phone and dialed Lacey's number.

"Hello?" Trent answered on the first ring.

I hesitated for a second. *Confident,* I reminded myself. "Hi, Trent. It's Kristin," I said.

"Oh, hey. I was just about to leave," Trent said.

"Well, that's why I'm calling," I said. My mind raced, trying to come up with a decent excuse for canceling our date. *Decisive,* I told myself. I decided not to lie. "There's this thing going on at the Manchester Club. My boyfriend is playing, and I really can't miss it. Sorry. I think Lacey's going with Richard, so if you want to go, maybe I'll see you there, okay?"

"Sure," Trent said. "No problem." He sounded a little confused but not upset or anything.

After I apologized again and said good-bye, I hung the phone back up and pulled off my new black sweater, flinging it on my bed. Then I dug my favorite cream-colored sweater with the pink scalloped neckline out of my dresser and pulled it on over my head. It felt soft and familiar, and it smelled like the laundry detergent my mom and I always use. I didn't have to look in the mirror.

I felt like me again.

Brian

"You guys are up next," Bette, the manager of the Manchester Club, told us. We were backstage, all ready to go. Or as ready as we'd ever be, under the circumstances. Bette pulled a stub of pencil out of her frizzy red hair and checked something off on her clipboard. "What's the name of your band again?" she asked me.

"Big Noise," I squeaked. I cleared my throat.

"I hope you're not the singer," Bette joked.

"That'd be me!" Salvador shouted, shadow boxing and dancing around like his underwear was too tight. "And I am sooo ready!" He laughed insanely. I guess that's how Salvador gets when he's nervous.

"Good luck," Bette said, raising her eyebrows at Blue and Damon like she felt sorry for them.

"We'll need it," Damon said grimly. His healthy, tan face was as pale as my sweat socks.

"Like, more than she knows," Blue agreed. He tapped his drumsticks together six times and then popped them behind his ears again. I'd already seen him do that very same thing about ten times in the last half hour. Talk about insane.

I put down my sax and walked over to where the black velvet curtain was hiding us from the audience and the stage. I was nervous. But not just about playing for the first time in front of a crowd. I pulled back the curtain and checked out the audience for about the thousandth time, searching for Kristin. The place was packed. Not just with kids from our school, but with every kid between the ages of twelve and fifteen in our whole county. Everyone was swaying to the mellow guitar music of this scruffy guy from Kennedy Middle School named Reed. I saw Jessica Wakefield, and Lacey Frells, and Richard Griggs, and Ginger Walters, and Matt Walker. But no Kristin. I felt like kicking myself.

Why hadn't I just sucked it up and talked to her about everything at school? I guess I was just hoping that she'd come tonight so that the new song could speak for itself. And maybe I thought that if I pretended the whole thing at Blue's house hadn't happened, it would just go away. More than anything, I guess I just chickened out.

I scanned the crowd again, hoping I'd made a mistake. She had to come. I hadn't put my band through all this trouble over a song for nothing.

So where was she?

Elizabeth

"Come on, Anna," I said, nudging her. "Let's go backstage and wish the guys good luck." Anna grabbed my hand. "Jessica, you coming?" I asked my sister. She was rocking back and forth and nodding her chin to this kid Reed's slow song. Jessica normally likes faster stuff, but Reed was a really good guitar player.

"Nuh-uh," Jessica said. "Damon said it would make him too nervous. I'll stay right here, though, so you can find me when you come back. Okay?"

"Okay," I said. Then I noticed a familiar face two girls away from Jessica. It was Lila Fowler, Jessica's former best friend at Sweet Valley Middle School and probably one of the snobbiest girls in Sweet Valley. I couldn't believe she was at the Manchester Club. The Lila Jessica and I knew wouldn't come to a place like this for fear of getting germs from the common people. Lila was wearing a yellow halter top, exposing her bare belly button. Maybe she had changed.

Elizabeth

"Don't look now, Jess," I whispered. "But Lila Fowler is standing right behind you."

Jessica tensed up and then cracked a little smile. "Well, that gives me something to do while you're gone," she said.

"You sure?" I asked. Lila and Jessica weren't exactly on good terms, not after Lila and her friends came and completely trashed our house during a party we'd had at the beginning of the school year.

"I'll be fine," Jessica said.

Anna and I wormed our way through the crowd, trying not to step on too many feet. We walked up the steps beside the stage. A woman with bright red, curly hair barred our way.

"You two playing tonight?" she asked us.

"No, we're just here to tell our friends good luck," Anna explained. "Big Noise. I think they're up soon."

"Aha," the woman said. "Groupies. Well, I don't usually let the audience back here, but those guys sure look like they could use some encouragement." She pulled the curtain aside. "Come on in."

"Thanks," Anna and I said, and we stepped behind the curtain.

Salvador, Blue, Brian, and Damon looked like they were about to be sick.

"Hi, guys," I said.

"Salvador," Anna said. "Did you eat dinner? You look kind of pale."

"Pale is in," Salvador said, wiping his forehead. "Pale is the new tan!" He didn't even laugh at his own joke like he usually does.

None of the other guys laughed either. Blue looked like a frightened reindeer with his drumsticks sticking out from behind his ears. Brian kept shifting his eyes behind me, like he expected the cops to come in and bust him for something. And Damon's fingers were twitching, like he was playing the guitar, except he wasn't holding his guitar.

I couldn't let them go onstage like this. I had to do something.

I grabbed Salvador's arm and pulled him to the side.

"Look, Sal," I said. "You've been acting really funny lately, and I know you're nervous, but you've got to get yourself together."

"Me? Nervous?" Salvador said. "I—"

"Shut up," I whispered. "Look, you're the lead singer of this band. You've got to act like it. You're my friend, and I love you, and I know you've got enough talent to blow everyone away. And so does the rest of the band. So get out there and prove it."

141

Elizabeth

"Really?" Salvador asked, the old familiar gleam in his gigantic black eyes.

"Yes, really," I said earnestly.

Salvador nodded and clapped as he walked backward, bumping into Brian. He suddenly looked like a different person. He turned to the other guys. "Listen, dudes," he said. "It's time to get out of this funk and get funky!" This time he laughed, and so did everyone else.

"Five minutes!" the red-haired woman called, poking her head around the curtain. "You girls might want to get back out there with your friends."

"Okay," I said.

"Hold on," Anna said. "Quick. Everyone down on all fours. This is a drama exercise. It really works."

Salvador, Blue, Brian, and Damon got down on all fours.

"Now growl," Anna instructed. "I mean it. Growl like a rabid dog. Really go for it."

"Grrr," the boys all growled.

"More!" Anna yelled at them.

"Grrrrrrrrrr!" Their lips were all turned up in a snarl, and they looked ridiculous. I knew that was the point of the exercise—letting go of your inhibitions.

Anna took my arm, and we walked quickly

142

off the stage. "Don't forget to breathe, you guys!" she called, and we ran away giggling before they could figure out what had happened to them.

"How did it go?" the woman with the red hair asked us as we headed back out into the screaming audience. Reed had stopped playing, and the crowd was hungry for more.

"They're ready," I told her.

Salvador

You're my friend, and I love you....

"Okay, boys," Bette yelled. "You're up!"

I didn't even look at the other guys. I just strutted onto the stage, hoping they would follow me.

They did. Blue sat down at the drums set up behind me. Damon fiddled with his guitar to my right. Brian took his place just to my left.

The room was packed with screaming girls. I cleared my throat, and they screamed even louder. I don't know what I'd been worried about. This was my dream come true.

I scanned the audience for one girl who probably wasn't screaming—it's not her style. *But she's my fan,* I told myself. *And I'm definitely her fan.* I wasn't completely deluded. I knew she liked Blue a lot. *But she loves me.*

I was ready to rock and roll!

"Okay. We're Big Noise," I said. The crowd went insane. "And we're going to play a song a good friend of mine helped me write while we were eating lunch."

Damon went into the wacky, futuristic guitar riff in the beginning of "Oreo Eyes." I couldn't see Elizabeth's face in the crowd anymore. I was too busy jumping up and down like a maniac, but I knew she was smiling. I was playing our song.

Kristin

"Excuse me, excuse me," I shouted at the bouncing, gyrating bodies all around me. Big Noise was just finishing up their first song, and I was trying to fight my way over to where Jessica and Lacey were dancing, strangely, side by side. That's the great thing about music, I guess. It brings people together.

"These guys are awesome!" Lacey shouted when I reached her. She had this huge smile on her face. *Wow*, I thought, *they must be really good.*

Jessica clutched my hand. "Damon is so cute! It's driving me crazy!" she screamed, and pointed at the stage. "Look at him!"

I raised my eyes and looked. But it wasn't Damon I noticed—it was Brian. His cheeks were all puffed up, and as he played the last few notes of the song on his sax, he leaned back, like he was really putting everything into it. Talk about cute. *Too bad he doesn't want to be my boyfriend anymore*, I thought bitterly.

The song ended with Salvador jumping up into a split in the air and shouting, "Shazam!" Everyone went crazy, clapping and screaming for more. Leave it to Salvador to work the crowd.

Salvador turned around to consult with his band mates for a second. They made a little huddle at the center of the stage. Then Salvador spun around, and Damon said into his mike, "Our buddy Brian wrote this song."

I steeled myself. Blue started to tap out the beat with his drumsticks, Salvador snapped his fingers to the beat, and Brian leaned forward into his mike and said, "This is for you, Kristin."

He didn't have to say that. I'd already heard the song. I knew it was meant for me. I just couldn't believe this was happening. Brian was breaking up with me in front of hundreds of dancing, screaming, happy people.

Then Salvador started to sing. "I saved you a place and the cheesiest slice, got you a diet soda in the brand that you like. Who else knows you this well? Who'd think of such things? Please think twice before you turn your back on me."

My breath caught in my throat. I started swaying, but not in time to the music. I was swooning.

147

It wasn't the same song. It was better. Much, much better.

"We're best friends, we meet after school; we talk on the phone, we say what we feel. . . ."

Salvador's voice was clear and sweet, but I wasn't looking at him. I couldn't take my eyes off Brian. He was playing his sax, and he was playing it for me.

I could tell.

Brian

I couldn't believe it. They loved us. We owned the crowd. We could do *anything*, and they'd scream for more. And even better, "Think Twice" was getting groovier by the minute. Salvador had picked up on the crowd's vibe—they were swaying and waving their lighters and giving us peace signs—and he'd gone into the extended remix version. We were kind of improvising, but it was all good. Seriously, at this point we could do no wrong.

I walked over to Salvador and started honking away on my sax like crazy. He bobbed his head and finished up the chorus for about the third time, and I riffed on into this major solo. I heard all these girls start screaming in the audience, and I had to force myself not to smile so I wouldn't lose my grip on my sax.

I couldn't believe it was all working out. Because if things had gone badly, it would have been because of me and all the trouble I caused over "Too Nice." Even if Kristin wasn't there to hear the song, I felt lucky. My band mates were really good guys. They deserved this.

I heard the same group of girls screaming at the top of their lungs. I picked them out of the crowd. And there was Kristin, right in the middle of the group, beaming up at me. And I could see by the look on her face that she'd already forgiven me. I wanted to drop my sax, run over to her, and tell her how sorry I was a million times, but I kept on playing. For her.

The feeling was amazing. It was better than I'd felt all week. Better, maybe, than I could ever remember feeling. It was partly because we were playing better than we ever had before. And it was partly because I had the best girlfriend in the entire universe. But mostly it was because I had my best friend back.

And on top of all that, I'd learned something really important.

Being nice is way underrated.

Check out the **all-new**....

(**Sweet Valley Web site**—)

www.sweetvalley.com

New Features

Cool Prizes

The **ONLY** official Web site!

Hot Links

(And much more!)

You hate your **alarm clock**.

You hate your **clothes**.

You're going to love Jr. High.